## Praise for *Down the Road*

"I enjoyed [*Down the Road*] very much . . . It's a helluva opening shot, and I look forward to more."
—Brian Keene, Bram Stoker Award–winning author of *The Rising* and *City of the Dead*

"A violent and relentless tale which pulls no punches, *Down the Road* will burn itself into your memory . . . This is pulp zombie fiction at its best. Written by a man who clearly loves the genre, the book is filled with nightmarish images and situations. Ibarra's bloody and visceral description of the disintegration of civilization is not only shocking and disturbing, but also uncomfortably plausible. This is a snapshot of a world gone mad where, free from the restraints of normality, both the living and the dead show their true colours. This is truly the end of the world."
—David Moody, author of *Hater*

"Nihilistic, tragic, oversexed and in many ways touching, Bowie Ibarra debuts with a real winner."
—John Hubbard, co-author of *Wandering Flesh* and contributing author in *The Undead Zombie Anthology*

"I thought [*Down the Road*] was a great read . . . I for one am looking forward to Bowie's next book. More zombies please!"
—Pain@allthingszombie.com

# DOWN the ROAD

## A Zombie Horror Story

## BOWIE IBARRA

GALLERY BOOKS

New York   London   Toronto   Sydney

Gallery Books
A Division of Simon & Schuster, Inc.
1230 Avenue of the Americas
New York, NY 10020

This book is a work of fiction. Names, characters, places, and incidents either are products of the author's imagination or are used fictitiously. Any resemblance to actual events or locales or persons, living or dead, is entirely coincidental.

First Gallery Books trade paperback edition January 2011

GALLERY BOOKS and colophon are trademarks of Simon & Schuster, Inc.

For information about special discounts for bulk purchases, please contact Simon & Schuster Special Sales at 1-866-506-1949 or business@simonandschuster.com.

The Simon & Schuster Speakers Bureau can bring authors to your live event. For more information or to book an event contact the Simon & Schuster Speakers Bureau at 1-866-248-3049 or visit our website at www.simonspeakers.com.

Manufactured in the United States of America

10  9  8  7  6  5  4  3  2  1

ISBN 978-1-4391-8069-3

# Introduction

## by Travis Adkins

Congratulations. You hold in your hands one of the coolest zombie novels ever written.

After I released my first zombie novel, *Twilight of the Dead*, I really started delving into other authors' works to see what else was out there. Bowie Ibarra's *Down the Road* was the first really good one that I stumbled across. His gritty narrative style and utter disregard for the sanctity of his characters was absolutely chilling. I mean, I was *unnerved* after I finished this book—and believe me, not since Stephen King's *The Long Walk* has a story stayed with me for so long.

*Down the Road* delivered in all the categories that I judge books by.

But alas, the author was the victim of an underachieving publisher and therefore his creative vision of *Down the Road* had not been fully realized. Readers could easily discern that the production quality of the novel was seriously lacking. So lacking, in fact, that the book wasn't receiving its due accolades.

Yet Bowie Ibarra stuck to his guns. After all, he knew he had created a pulp zombie masterpiece and it was only a matter of time before the right people took notice.

And then the right people *did*.

In my opinion, Bowie Ibarra is the Quentin Tarantino of zombie literature. He fully understands what readers appreciate in a zombie tale and goes balls-to-the-wall to put it into words. Simply put, he knows what makes a book *fun*. Descriptive gore, action, drama, suspense, erotica and clever dialogue—these elements are all present and accounted for in *Down the Road*. It's truly everything you could ask for in a tale of the zombieverse.

I also need to comment on the author's exploration of emergency management in times of crisis. George Romero, in his classic *Night of the Living Dead*, was the first person to coin the phrase, "Rescue Stations." And ever since, those words have become a staple in zombie lore, a base element from which zombie literature expands. Nearly every writer in the genre (even me, admittedly) casually tosses around the words "Rescue Station."

A rescue station is usually just that, and nothing more.

Bowie Ibarra, however, takes the concept one step further. His nightmarish vision of FEMA camps was at first shunned by some of his critics. "Those things would never happen," they said. "Racial segregation, rapes, murders, a half-assed government response, overbearing power trips by the military? Nope. It would never happen. Not in this country."

Well, in the aftermath of Hurricane Katrina, it's quite obvious that Bowie's interpretation of FEMA camps is not so farfetched. And here he was describing FEMA procedures while many of us didn't even know what the acronym stood for. (Me again.)

Can you say, "visionary"?

These things *happen*. They really do.

Every fan of the zombie genre wonders just how in the hell humanity could lose in the face of such slow-walking monstrosities. Well, when the dead rise and start to eat the living (it will happen someday; you'd better believe it) I think it's quite obvious now that FEMA camps and "Rescue Stations" will play an integral role in humanity's downfall.

I thank you, Mr. Ibarra, for the heads-up.

Now out from under the smothering heel of his former publisher and in the highly capable hands of Permuted Press, Bowie Ibarra's definitive vision of *Down the Road* has been realized.

Here's to you, my friend. Your work is perfect pulp zombie fiction. It successfully encompasses everything an undead acolyte appreciates, making for a truly enjoyable reading experience.

Now, dear reader, you're free to begin Bowie Ibarra's *Down the Road: A Zombie Horror Story*.

And hopefully the flesh-eaters contained herein will *stay* contained herein.

(You'd best lock your doors and board up your windows just to be safe.)

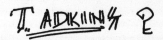

*This book is first and foremost dedicated to George A. Romero*

# Chapter 1

"Current reports show that the mystery illness that struck New York City one week ago has now spread across the country. The unknown disease has now been reported in all states in the continental United States. The sickness has not been reported as of yet in Alaska and Hawaii. Doris West has more . . ."

George Zaragosa was listening to the report as he packed his bag. The trip wasn't going to be easy, and since he wouldn't have any place to change until he made it, he filled his sturdy black travel bag only with canned goods. Mostly beans. As a single guy, George wasn't much for cooking. The one thing he *could* cook (and cook well) was chalupas, which merely consisted of warming up the beans. The beans for the chalupas were about the only canned goods he ever bought, apart from beer.

"The illness that begins with a strong fever resulting in death within hours has spread across the nation," said Doris West, whose sultry voice was placed over news footage of hospital beds in New York City. Images of doctors and nurses working frantically to take care of the sick filled the screen. "Doctors and public officials are at a loss as to how to contain the growing threat."

"All the hospitals on the Island are now filled to capacity, and several of the boroughs are reporting the same," said Dr. Richard Hammond, who looked visibly exhausted. "We're having to turn people away. Fortunately, FEMA recently began opening centers around town to help those we're turning away."

*Helpful FEMA centers,* George thought. *Sounds like an oxymoron to me.*

George had a healthy distrust of the people running the U.S. government, especially the agencies like the Federal Emergency Management Agency and the Bureau of Alcohol, Tobacco and Firearms. The actions of FEMA at the Seattle riots and the bad choices of the BATF at Waco and Ruby Ridge didn't inspire any semblance of confidence in George for those agencies, especially for the people that ran them.

George packed his pistol, a simple .38 Special with enough ammunition to last longer than the food. His gut churned at the thought of having to use it.

*But I guess that's what I bought it for,* he figured.

Years ago, he remembered shooting at the rifle range with his dad back in his hometown of San Uvalde. He was young and not too interested, but he was taught the ins and outs of gun responsibility. One of the comments that always stuck in his head was when his dad told him, "If you're going to own a gun, you'd better be prepared to use it." With that thought in his head, it took him several years to finally purchase one, but the decision was easy. With break-ins becoming a problem in his apartment complex, he knew he wanted to be able to protect his property.

"What emergency management personnel are now investigating is why New York wasn't the only area infected," Doris chimed in over images of bodies being carried out of hospitals. "A day later, Los Angeles, Dallas, Miami, Chicago, Minneapolis, Seattle, and Washington D.C. were all exposed to horrendous outbreaks of the illness. Government officials have not ruled out a biological attack from terrorists, and the FBI and CIA are currently investigating. No groups have come forward to claim responsibility."

The irony of even owning the gun now to protect his property was obvious to George as he looked around his sparsely lit one room apartment. He looked at his computer and knew it probably wouldn't be here if and when he came back. Looters had been a problem in Austin for the past three days since the "State of Emergency" was declared two days before. Schools closed, stores boarded up their windows, and FEMA centers opened. Surprisingly, the FEMA centers were very well prepared for the city going ape.

But the local police could barely get a handle on the various problems rising around the city, especially looters. Half the cops were busy fighting the hordes of mysterious undead creatures that had suddenly taken over the poorer neighborhoods. Another small yet noticeable portion of the police had headed to the hills with their families. With the force that was left, the south side didn't get quite as much protection as the well-to-do north side.

Naturally.

Unfortunately, that was also the side of town George lived on. Sirens, gunshots, and screams serenaded him to sleep for the last two nights since the outbreak. It was obvious public safety was slowly being thrown to the wayside.

The police dressed like armored Nazi stormtroopers didn't help either. They were working openly with the military under the guise of "Homeland Security."

Coming out of his daydream for a moment, George looked around the room again, trying to figure out what to take. The movies he had begun to collect would also disappear. His favorite movies including *Raiders of the Lost Ark* and *The Big Lebowski* would be gone. It made him think how lucky he was to actually have all of those items, as well as everything else in his room. It was probably a safe bet that he wouldn't have another bed to sleep in for a while, even if he made it home.

"Matters became more complicated as a frightening trend began to emerge. Three days ago, in the early morning, everything was fine. Then by the afternoon, several dead patients began to rise," explained a nurse, her uniform so soiled that it was too much of a distraction for George to catch her name, which had flashed momentarily across the bottom of the screen. "We thought it was a mistake, at first, a misdiagnosis of them being dead. But as they began to attack staff members, we knew something was wrong."

"By seven o'clock that evening, two floors of a hospital in New York City had been locked down and patients moved to different floors," added Doris West. Footage of medical staff relocating their patients was displayed on screen for a moment, effectively narrated, then those images were removed and Doris was shown again. "Other hospitals were soon to follow suit.

"Funeral Directors reported the same activity at morgues around the city."

". . . Body bags began moving . . . moaning . . . we didn't know what to do. They were dead when we picked them up," stated mortician Steve Alexander, "The problem is the same here. We've had to shut this place down and lock it up."

"Early reports had at least one hundred to two hundred people showing up at local hospitals across the east coast within hours of the first report. And within hours, those people died. Doctors hadn't even had enough time to diagnose the problem. A majority expired in the waiting room.

"That was three days ago."

The one thing George was going to miss was his compact disc music collection. Losing that was really going to hurt. Music was important to him—an inspiration even—and it showed in his library of custom-made tapes, reflecting different moods he would experience day by day.

It was at that point that George felt a tinge of helplessness. Sure, he had accumulated such comforts as he tried to make a living for himself teaching children about theatre in the nearby town of Koehl, but now he knew nothing could save his apartment—an apartment he hadn't been renting for even a year yet.

He knew one thing, though. He needed to get out of the city, apartment be damned.

"The fact of the matter is that within hours, the bodies of the recently deceased began to rise. A violent and what most have described as a cannibalistic impulse seemed to overtake the bodies as they started to attack and devour the living," said a police chief in Miami. "We're not sure how to contain them."

"Though these creatures have attacked the living, there have been no reports of the creatures attacking each other," Doris said over images of confused hospital technicians and sick patients, of confused crowds in the streets by hospitals, and then of a young woman holding her grandmother, both of them crying. "However, there are claims that bites from the creatures are leading to more infections."

The television showed a camera taking in the image of a woman running across a busy street, helped by a friend. Her arm had a very noticeable bite wound and was bleeding quite a lot of blood.

"The fact remains that across the country, people are dying. And those people are somehow coming back to life. Doris West, News Four, Austin."

Zipping up his bag, George took one last look around his apartment. *I guess I won't have to worry about rent for a while*, he joked to himself.

It wasn't much of a joke, though. George was scared. It would have been much easier for him to stay locked up in his apartment until this problem got under some sort of control. He had food that could last at least a few weeks if he wasn't wasteful. He would certainly be home, back to San Uvalde, by then.

"Thank you, Doris," said the news anchor in his three-piece blue suit. "Homeland Security has issued another emergency notification for the Austin public at large." A ticker at the bottom of the screen started listing off locations of FEMA centers around Austin.

*Home.* He was going to go home. He was going to survive this mess and make it home—at least that's what the optimist in him had told him. The truth was it had been three days already and the problem was still spreading across the country. When the first reports came in, George couldn't believe his ears. A day after the first reports outside of Texas, an early morning news show broke the story of the first reanimation in Austin. George had just woken up and was preparing for school, and was watching the morning news, the same news program that he watched every morning. That same day several hours later, twenty-four people had been attacked by the creatures. All were infected. All twenty-four died and came back to life mere hours after infection. It was around that time that the sick began to fill the beds of Austin area hospitals, all on their last leg.

"All citizens are to report to any of the following FEMA centers nearest where you live: Bowie High School, Crockett High School, Travis High School, YMCA central . . ."

School was a bit nerve-wracking as the first reports were coming in. No one had really responded to the crisis in Koehl and the absence rate was about the same. However, things would change by the end of the day.

By the time he had arrived home from work that day, just two days ago, the death toll had already reached a thousand plus, with over a thousand more infected. By the end of the next workday, the Austin area hospitals had been pushed to their limits. The absences were alarmingly high that day at school. George had one class with only five students. None of them wanted to be there, especially after the rumors circulated that a coach had beat down one of the creatures with a football helmet before school started that morning.

The creature was rumored to be the grandmother of one of George's students, who died the day before.

"...Leander Public High School, Dripping Springs High School, Wimberlay Volunteer Fire Department, Wimberlay High School..."

Schools around the country were closing. The district was staying open, considering the threat and when, exactly, to do the same. The district was going to squeeze every last dime from the state for attendance. The district was very good about sending e-mails to update the faculty and staff of the situation in Hayes County. Eventually, the wish to cancel school came true.

School was let out at lunch that second day and would be out indefinitely. But before George could get home, his supervisor, Assistant Principal Ross Raymond, pulled him aside.

"George, we've had a complaint from a student that you were rough with him?"

"What?" This was clearly a conversation that could wait for later, considering the circumstances.

"He said you yanked him by the arm in class. It left a bruise."

George was upset. "Ross, listen. Did the kid tell you that he was trying to walk out of my class during the incident with the football coach? Ya'll had just announced not to let kids out of the room."

Ross was just as tense as George, and chose to postpone

the discussion. "Listen, George, when school starts back up again, we need to talk about this. I don't know the whole story yet, but at this point you might be suspended."

George wanted to fly off the handle. After teaching for ten years, this felt like a slap in the face.

That was when he decided he needed to get home. He would risk the large amount of traffic that had begun to pack the interstate.

*Enough of this crap,* George thought. *No more TV.*

As he walked toward the bed where the remote for the TV was, he glanced up at the picture on the wall. It was a photo of him and his deceased fiancée. Her name was Esparanza Garcia, and he loved her.

Taking a moment, George remembered the day they first met. He was in line at the theater, waiting to buy a ticket for some pirate movie his friends had suggested. Not having any luck for a date, George was going solo, but that never bothered him. George was used to being alone. In a way, he preferred it. He liked to do his own thing.

A few moments later, Esparanza was standing in line with two other female friends. His attention was grabbed by her choice of fragrance, *il bacio,* and George turned. He didn't know what the spark was or if it was some fat angel with an arrow, but he was enraptured nonetheless. She smiled. He smiled. A year later, George proposed to her in line at the movies, the very same place and time they had met.

George took the picture from the wall and carefully removed the photo from its frame, relocating it to his wallet. It was the first time he had ever put a picture in his wallet.

9

Ready to go, George grabbed the remote to turn off the television. In his haste, his hand brushed against the "last channel" button. The television switched to PBS.

"Hmpf," George grunted, "*Sesame Street.*"

Big Bird was trying to coax Oscar the Grouch to help pronounce a word with the letter "G." Good old Oscar, being the Grouch that he was, was being a pain in the ass by refusing to say the word. The only evidence that the program was in any way affected by the plague was the ticker on the bottom of the screen showing the names of school cancellations.

*C'mon, Oscar,* George mused. *It's your own goddamn last name. Just read it.*

He switched off the television.

Before he walked out of his apartment for the last time, George grabbed one of his custom tapes that was on the floor by the door. It was his "Fightin' Music" tape, filled with music that inspired him to combat. It was used during his high school football days to fire him up before a game. If today was a football game, it was 1st and 10 with two-hundred-some odd miles to go. San Uvalde was the goal line. It used to be a simple two-and-a-half hour drive on a Saturday morning. Now it looked like it might take a little bit longer to get down the road.

George's black ultra-lite boots were comfortable, as were his faded blue Wranglers. He put on his red and black checkered flannel over his "APA Protection" T-shirt and picked up his bag.

George closed the door behind him.

He didn't bother to lock it.

# Chapter 2

Looking out over the patio area of the third floor, George caught a glimpse of some neighbors down the street packing their goods into the back of a U-Haul. The parking lot, in general, was particularly barren. Even though most of the tenants would be clocking out at around this time from their lower middle-class jobs, the sparseness of automobiles in the parking lot sent a grave feeling through George's mind.

*Maybe I'm late! Maybe everyone has already left, and I'm late!*

Machine-gun fire in the shopping center next to the apartment complex shook George back to reality. "Just get moving, dumbass," he said aloud. He began descending the stairway. His bag hung from his right hand, a little heavy, but not enough to hamper him.

As George hit the bottom of the stairway, something hit his nose like a brick—or more like a brick shithouse. It reeked, bad. George gagged as he stepped back up the stairs to avoid the stench.

"What the hell is that?!" he exclaimed, lifting his black shirt to cover his nose. The odor stunk like a stack of dead animals, or like a homeless guy sitting on the side of the street—the kind with the *I'm not going to lie, I want a beer* signs. George hated those unfortunate bastards.

But it wasn't the same stench. It was something else. It took a quick glance toward the parking lot to his right for George to figure out where the stench was coming from. Walking across the lot, between the buildings, was a slow-moving ragged person. It looked like a homeless guy, in all honesty, but the walk was something different. The person walked in a slow stagger, rocking back and forth as it stepped.

As his pulse began to quicken, George knew that the figure was one of those creatures, the ones the news that the rest of the nation was crapping their collective pants over. He had now seen his first living dead creature, and it fascinated him.

*How the hell are these broke-down, slow pieces of crap taking this nation by the balls?* he wondered.

He put down his gear and slowly began moving toward the creature.

"I can take this one," he stated with bravado. "Let's see what all the fuss is about."

Walking down the sidewalk between the buildings to his right and left, and the lots in front and behind him, George noticed the stench getting stronger. "Damn, you're one stinky motherfucker," he muttered. He took a moment and looked at the apartment doors to his right and left. On the right side the door was wide open, but it appeared to have been looted. He wasn't going to go near it.

"I can do this," he reassured himself. "I'm better than them."

Then, as George turned to his left a creature grabbed him around the waist and ungracefully tackled him, bringing him to the ground. He hadn't even seen it—it must have been hiding in the doorway to his left.

*The sneaky fucker.*

George and the creature both landed with an awkward thud. George let out a loud scream, but caught his breath and began to scramble on the ground, breaking the grip that was surprisingly strong around his waist. Adrenaline and fear pulsed through his veins.

George was surprised at his instinct. It was a simple counter to a waist lock that he had learned in college while taking a basic amateur wrestling class. George took many martial arts classes, with western boxing being his most proficient skill, even though he lost a controversial decision at a boxing toughman competition held by the university fraternities. He had trained very hard for the fight and mixed it up well, but he felt he had been set up as a patsy for some juiced-up fraternity type.

Even though he had extensive training in western boxing, the wrestling still stood out to him mostly because he wished he had taken it longer.

The wrestling instructor, a short, goateed man named Sam Eaker, taught the counter on the first day of his class. It was a basic move—*a valuable move*—but George remembered how inefficient it seemed at the time. The maneuver seemed too slow and kind of looked like something professional wrestlers would do.

And *that* was hardly practical.

However, today, it worked. And it might have helped that his current opponent wasn't nearly as agile as a living person.

Making his way to his feet, George swiftly turned around. Though the monster had been tricky getting George to the ground, it was struggling just to regain its footing.

With intention, George reeled back his foot and delivered a massive kick to the creature's mouth with his heavy black boot. The creature's jaw repositioned itself and its mouth became a bloody mess as several teeth fell to the pavement and clattered across the concrete like dice rolled by a street hustler. Soon after, its head smacked the ground.

The ghoul flinched, but then tried to bring itself to its feet again. Raising his right foot, George maliciously stomped on its head, forcing it to smack against the sidewalk. The creature flinched again and tried to move, but George followed up with five more stomps to the head and face, the fifth bringing a cracking sound to his ears. Curb stomping without the curb.

The ghoul didn't move after that.

Looking up, George noticed that he had caught the attention of the homeless creature and it was making its way to him.

*Way to go, stupid,* thought George, as the creature continued to amble forward like a drunken wino who had had too much Ripple or Thunderbird.

He wasn't going to take another foolish risk. He knew he was good and could handle himself in a fight, but now he realized with certainty exactly why the nationwide crisis was getting out of control. After all, all it took was one bite from a dead creature—*one lucky bite*—and another poor soul was infected, destined to become one of them. He wondered how many people had faced one of the creatures with the cocky bravado he just had, only to not be as lucky as he was.

George ran back to the stairway, got his gear, and carefully strode to his car, his eyes constantly surveying the lot for danger.

All clear.

# Chapter 3

George put the key in the ignition and started the vehicle, his gear having been stuffed hastily in the back seat. The car was a black 1993 two door Chevy Cavalier. It was a dependable vehicle, getting him through college and beyond, and held quite a lot of sentimental value. Though the paint was beginning to fade and the tape deck was not what the factory installed, George held his vehicle in high regard, even going so far as to christen it, "The Chevalier." It was a silly play on words, combing the make and model. He thought it was an actual word, like a French knight, but wasn't sure. The vehicle had made that journey down the road to San Uvalde many times before, whether it was from Beeville near the Texas coast, Canyon up in the Texas panhandle, or San Marcos where George finished his schooling.

"All right, bud," whispered George, "Do it one more time."

As the car warmed up, George looked in the rearview mirror. The homeless creature was halfway down the path where the scuffle had taken place, shuffling toward the vehicle. Far enough away that George was safe, but close enough to give him the chills.

He pushed in the clutch and shifted into reverse. The Cavalier glided backward, and shifting into first gear, George directed the "black knight" to the front gate of the apartment complex.

As he drove to the gate, he switched on the radio. A stern male voice boomed through the speakers.

". . . No longer allowed to seek occupancy in any private residence or property anywhere. Citizens found to be occupying private residences will be fined and incarcerated."

*Bastards*, thought George. *Looks like FEMA and Homeland Security utilized the black box.*

The black box was a device all radio stations were required to have installed into their main system by the FCC. The box allowed FEMA and the federal government to immediately requisition every radio station with these boxes during a state of emergency. Once utilized, they would relay messages to the masses about what they need to do next. He didn't expect the messages to be so menacing.

*And people thought FEMA camps were a joke*, he mused. *Rex-84, people.*

"Once again, citizens are to report to the FEMA center in or near their place of residence. A state of emergency has been declared by Homeland Security across the nation. You are no longer allowed to seek occupancy in any private residence or property anywhere, regardless of how safe you might be. Citizens found to be occupying private residences will be fined and incarcerated."

"*Incarcerated,*" George echoed. "Sounds the same as being in a FEMA camp to me. What a crock of shit."

One of George's friends, Bogart Sylvan, once commented to George that he sure did cuss a lot for being a school teacher. In a way, Bogart was right. However, George was the consummate gentleman and teacher at school and—for the most part—in public. A teacher's reputation is always secretly scrutinized by the world around them, including their own colleagues. However, on this day, George was alone and always allowed himself to express the fear and anger he sometimes held inside himself. George was, by nature, a kindhearted person, but holding in frustrations from disrespectful students, work pressures, and broken relationships made for an always tense George Zaragosa. His possible suspension from work did nothing to ease that tension, either.

With the gate wide open now, George shifted to first and put his foot on the accelerator and turned the corner toward the highway.

"Holy shit," he mouthed as he looked out onto the interstate and adjoining access road, both of which were congested with cars leaving Austin. Some were staying in line. Others were blazing their own trail. He gritted, "I ain't got time for this," as he pulled onto the access road.

"The only safety for you and your family is in the nearest FEMA center in your area. We cannot stress this enough. The FEMA center is equipped to protect and provide for you and your family while this crisis is contained by members of Homeland Security."

"Contained," mocked George. "Whatever."

"The bodies of the recently deceased are returning to life and attacking the living. If you are approached by one of these creatures, there are simple measures that can be utilized to protect yourself. Blunt trauma to the head or spine or a gunshot to the head or spine will immobilize the monster. You are discouraged, though, from using a firearm within the city limits, and are subject to local and federal laws regarding firearms if you choose to use a firearm to immobilize a creature. If local law enforcement or members of Homeland Security find firearms while securing your family from your property, you will be subject to possible interrogation and incarceration."

"Goddamn! What a load of shit!" George shouted. He flicked off the radio in disgust and slid one of his mix tapes into the tape player. It was his classical music mix. Albinoni's "Adagio" began to play as he continued down the road.

The cars were moving, but in a very erratic fashion. However, at least they *were* moving. As George drove, he noticed just down the way that several vehicles had stopped after a small fender-bender.

*What the hell are they stopping for,* he wondered. *They're crazy if they want the cops to sort this out.*

Looking into the ditch between the highway and the access road, George saw an overturned Chevy Blazer. Luggage was strewn around the vehicle. The driver, a blond guy in a blue shirt and slacks, was scratching his head while his three passengers were trying to roll the vehicle right side up again.

*Good luck with that,* he thought.

Two sets of lights were flashing off to the left of George near the concrete median in the middle of the interstate. They were Austin police cars. Looking closer, he noticed they were empty.

*What's that all about?*

As he came over the hill, George saw that on the highway an eighteen-wheeler was overturned, smoke rising from its underbelly. Traffic began to slow a bit in his lane until it came to a stop.

"Dammit," he mouthed, steaming. He squinted his eyes to try to see farther ahead, and that was when he saw two policemen—probably the same ones from the empty cruiser—walking between cars, issuing tickets to drivers. Some drivers were leaning out their windows, obviously cursing, while others were taking their tickets passively as if they saw no other option.

*Fucking unbelievable.*

George looked to the side of the road. Several cars were lined up along the shoulder. Beside the cars were people sitting in handcuffs. Two small children were also in bonds.

"What the fuck is this shit," said George as he looked back toward the cops for an explanation. Watching one of them, he noticed money changing hands. "Oh, what a horse-drawn carriage of bullshit!" he gritted. The cops seemed to be demanding payments for the tickets immediately. If you didn't have the cash, they were sending you to jail.

He stopped his car and waited for them to approach. He rolled down his window.

Next to him on his left was a large Dodge Ram. It was maroon, jacked up somewhat on some big wheels, and had a fierce metal grill guard on the front with a winch. It was one of those gas-guzzling vehicles, the ones environmentalists twisted their panties in knots over.

George noticed that that vehicle's window was also rolled down. The driver, clearly an out-of-place shitkicker with a worn cowboy hat, sat glum-faced and frustrated.

George called to him, "What a load of bullshit, huh?!"

The driver looked over, and without missing a beat, replied, "You're telling me. I don't have any money for these cocksuckers. My family's waiting for me in Koehl. We're heading into the hills. Homeland Security doesn't make me feel so secure with their machine guns and all, and I'm not much for this FEMA center idea."

"Me either," George replied. He faced forward again and sighed. He had *some* cash, more along the lines of pocket money, but he certainly wasn't going to give it to those thugs.

The cops were about four cars down now.

"I'm George Zaragosa."

"Steve Whitten. Nice to meet you, man."

"Likewise."

Steve slapped at his steering wheel in frustration as his machine burned more fuel. "I'm all for following the law, but this is different. Nothing like this has ever happened before."

The cops moved to about three cars down from George and began taking down information. The line of cars were moving slowly. On the highway, it was the same story. Everyone was trying to work their way into the one open lane to get around the rig.

"Where'd you come from?" asked George.

"Man, I went into the H.E.B. to get some water. Got the last of it. I paid for mine, but a lot of people were just walking out. No security, and a lot of the employees were getting roughed up. They're kind of letting people get away with it. I'm surprised anyone is working to begin with. It's crazy over there, but this ticket thing right now is crazier. What's the purpose of this? Like any of these people even care anymore . . ."

A thought came to George's head, fueled by the current actions of the police, that was aggravating him beyond belief. He ranted, "Man, we can't let these people take advantage of us anymore. This is fucking bullshit! They're still in their revenue-generation mindset! Hell, it's an outright mugging if you ask me!"

"I hear you, man," agreed Steve, sulking.

"Hey, you need to get to your family, right?"

"Well, yeah."

"And you know heading for the hills will make you a criminal, right?"

The guy thought for a minute, then replied, "Well, they say they're going to fine us."

"Fine you? Hell, if they find you out there, who knows what they'd do to you and your family."

"You might be right."

George knew he was. The way the local police had already been SWAT-teaming the city and neutralizing some of the zombies, but—*curiously enough*—securing whole neighborhoods and turning them into veritable prison camps, he knew when they went hunting for people staying in their own homes it wasn't going to be so nice.

George took a long, hard moment before stating with finality, "Listen man, I need to get home to my family, too. We don't have time for this." Butterflies were swarming in his stomach. It was making him sick to suggest what he was suggesting. He said in a hush, "*We need to make a break for it.*"

"Uh, what the hell do you mean?" Steve asked, obviously not wanting to say out loud what he knew George was suggesting.

"There's just two of them," George said, very anxious now. Adrenaline began coursing through his veins. His body was hot. His vision was narrow. "I can hit them both if we take off now. It's a clearer shot down this road once we pass them since they've slowed things down. If we go now, we can get onto the interstate when we pass the rig on the highway."

"I don't know, man," Steve said. Doubt echoed in his voice, but George's matter-of-fact logic was somehow making a lot of sense. "What about the cops?"

"Fuck the cops, man," said George, "They're not going to give a shit when they find you in the hills!" George's anger was showing on his face. He had already convinced *himself*, and was determined now to follow through. "Look, you need to get to your family and so do I . . . But we've got to go *now!*"

Several seconds passed, during which George saw Steve's lips stuttering as they tried to give voice to his reply.

*He's not going to do it,* George thought.

Suddenly, Steve put his truck in gear and backed up, eyes wide and engine roaring. His solid iron bumper pushed the Dodge Neon behind it backward, screwing up its front end quite badly. The driver of the Neon honked several times in quick, angry succession.

"Let's do this," Steve growled, his face carved out of stone.

George nodded and switched his car in gear and gunned it, got out of line, and aimed right at both officers who were now standing by two separate cars, one in front of the other in a perfect line. Steve took out the back end of the car in front of George, then waited for George to go ahead and followed right behind his black Cavalier.

The first cop didn't know what hit him as the front of the low-set Cavalier took his legs out from under him. Both his knees were blown out, tendons and ligaments snapping as one part of his body went under the vehicle, bending in ways it was never meant to bend. A loud scream emanated from the policeman's throat, but was cut short as the vehicle advanced. His spine snapped at the waist and his upper body slammed against the black Cavalier, face first, leaving a large dent and a small patch of blood on the hood. His body was then immediately swallowed under the car. For a few feet, the body became stuck under the vehicle and was dragged across the pavement. The car and road both chewed at the body. Flesh and clothes began to tear against the gravel, his right arm snapped off at the shoulder, allowing the body to free itself from the pseudo-grinder and exit behind the vehicle. Steve's truck finished the job, crushing the cop's legs under its massive right wheels.

The second cop turned and watched his partner get creamed by the black Cavalier. His eyes opened wide and his mouth was agape under his dark, full moustache. For a moment he was frozen as the black death-dealer wheeled his way toward him. It was seconds away before his instincts took over. Bending at the knees, he quickly sprang into the air. The Cavalier clipped his ankles, causing him to spin like a fan as he flew over the hood of the vehicle he was ticketing. George briefly scraped the other vehicle, a forest-green Nissan Maxima, and advanced down the road. The cop hit the ground on the other side of the vehicle, his ankles bent backward as Steve's large truck sped past. The passenger in the Maxima, a middle-aged blond woman, rolled down her window. She yelled, "Asshole!" The cop slowly got to his knees, pulled out his pistol, and tried to get a clear shot at the renegade vehicles.

However, before he could get a clear shot, all the vehicles behind him—seeing the action in front of them and realizing the opportunity—began a vehicular bum rush of the guards of the makeshift checkpoint. Even the middle-aged blond woman seized the moment and joined the pack. The cop got a futile shot off before he had to flee to the relative safety of the freeway and back to his vehicle, limping and hobbling. It seemed like the checkered flag had unleashed a group of race cars as the access road became a speedway. Cars bumped into each other and tempers flared as the once stalled line of cars were in motion, going their own ways down the road. The dam had broken, and George's fellow Austinites were on their way.

The road past the ticket trap was clear, and once George passed the overturned rig on the highway via the access road, he found a level section of the grassy median and crossed over onto the relatively uncongested highway. Steve was right behind. The others were right behind Steve.

George and Steve bounded onto the road. Adrenaline still coursed through George's veins. There was a bit of fear and anticipation working its way through his mind, but he ignored it. He knew, somehow, this was only the beginning.

Steve pulled up beside George as they sped down the road. With a rebel yell, Steve told him, "You're a bad man, George! But you da man! You got us out of there!"

"No problem!" George yelled back. "I'll follow you to Buda."

"If you want—but it's crazy there! Lots of those monsters around!"

George knew the story. "I got you, man! I'm ready!"

George slowed down a bit to get behind the maroon juggernaut, a defiant convoy of two.

He was quiet, for the most part, as he listened to his classical music.

He didn't want to think too much about what he'd just done, about the faces of the two policemen, both young-looking, both run down for following orders given by authority figures who had probably long deserted their posts. He didn't want to think about any wives or children the officers might have had at home or in the FEMA centers, or of the family they wouldn't see again.

After all, George had a family too.

He had to make priorities.

He turned the music up louder, and continued down the road.

They were making pretty good time as Steve's big maroon truck blazed a trail down IH-35. It would only be about fifteen minutes before George arrived back at his school when it hit him:

"Aw, shit!" he exclaimed, punching the steering wheel with his fists. He had forgotten the keys to the building back at his apartment. "Goddammit! How the hell am I going to get in?!"

He'd have to break in now, he knew. But how?

At this point, it didn't matter.

It was her gift to him. He had to get it back.

He didn't know why he absolutely needed to return to work to get it. It certainly wasn't safe there, not now, and not with the time it might take to get home. But he knew he had to retrieve it. It was all he had left of her.

George had taken the small gift, a gold crucifix necklace, to school for a show-and-tell project for his theater class. The idea was to show how bringing something to a scene can make the scene much more meaningful and powerful. He acted out the monologue from a noir-style detective play about a pink gun, using the necklace as a prop. It was a monologue about how the character, Dwayne Stark, had lost his wife to a murderer. When he first performed the monologue, it had some meaning to it. But when he used the crucifix, it brought a lot more.

There was a reason for that.

George had lost his fiancée six months earlier.

# Chapter 4

Six months ago, Esparanza Garcia, George's fiancée, was found dead in a back alley. Blunt head trauma and two gunshot wounds to the back. Her murder was labeled as a "drug deal gone bad" by authorities, but George knew there had to be more to it.

Esparanza was by no means into drugs at all. She did enjoy a White Russian or a Tanqueray and soda every once in a while, but she never did drugs.

And that's what she told that man. His name was Alphonso Gonzalez. Alphonso was hiring guards from a security agency that Esparanza was working for. He was a smart and handsome man from Mexico. He had all the qualities a young woman like Esparanza should have loved. When Alphonso would visit, he would promise her the world, playfully, but with meaning. Esparanza would always graciously, perhaps coquettishly, refuse. George learned about this later, but never gave it much mind. Unlike Esparanza, George was not jealous. He trusted his woman. Esparanza was denying the man, so there was no harm in a little flirting. She *was* beautiful, after all, and a little simple flirting could probably defuse an otherwise volatile situation.

She had long black hair and a soft, shapely body. She had the kind of strength gained from hours at the gym and the conditioning of a dancer. Her round face and pretty smile complemented her big brown eyes. She had a charm to her—a charm she had learned to use to her advantage.

Alphonso could get anything for Esparanza, and Esparanza wanted a lot of stuff—land, a good car, a baby. However, she would have to pay a price if she wanted it from Alphonso, and it was a price she had no idea she would have to pay.

One day Alphonso repeated one of his many offers to hire Esparanza to work for him. She gave in this time, deciding to give it a chance. Anything would be better than the pay she was receiving, and Alphonso promised it would be much more.

Esparanza walked into Alphonso's office later that afternoon. She was wearing her black work pants and shoes with a comfortable white blouse. Alphonso looked suave, wearing his trademark gray suit with a black shirt underneath.

Conversation up to that point had been amicable and pleasant. Esparanza even told a blond joke she had read from an e-mail she received earlier that afternoon.

But things quickly turned dangerously aggressive as Alphonso began to insinuate she was a narc.

"Why do you think that?" Esparanza asked, a confused and frightened look on her face. "I thought you were offering me a job?"

"You can't be that good," replied Alphonso as he reached into a filing cabinet near his desk.

"What are you talking about? Why are you being mean to me?"

"Do you know why you're here?"

Esparanza shook her head no.

"Why don't you sit down?" Alphonso offered her a chair near the middle of the long executive business table. She took a seat, fear and uncertainty beginning to overwhelm her.

"If you want to be set for life, just say yes to me. Join me, my dear," Alphonso suavely stated, standing directly behind her.

"I don't love you, though," she said defiantly, a clear scoff in her voice. She didn't even bother to turn around and face him. "I love George and you know that. We're engaged."

"What can he get for you? Nothing and you know it! A school teacher? He's a slave just like everyone else. An indentured servant to a bankrupt system. Maybe his retirement will actually be worth something in thirty years. Hell, the superintendent of the district helps me with my business ventures. I could put in a good word."

"I don't love you," she said again. Tears began forming on her lower eyelids. She blinked them away.

"You really are an innocent bitch, aren't you? I don't believe it."

Alphonso pulled out a manila folder and threw the contents onto the table. On top was a picture of Esparanza's mother exiting a local convenience store. Next to it was a picture of her little brother, Elias, swinging on the monkey bars at school. Yet another was a picture of George's mother exiting her house in San Uvalde, a town miles away from Austin. Another was a picture of George at work.

"What is this?" asked Esparanza, completely taken off guard by the photos.

"These are examples of how you can never get away from me if you're lying." He put his finger down on a tape recorder and played back a conversation between herself and George.

"What is this?" she asked again, coming to terms with a startling realization. "What is it exactly that you do?"

Alphonso chuckled a bit before replying, "Let's just say I help members of our community escape the daily grind."

Esparanza fought to hold back her tears. She knew she should have seen this coming.

"I want to leave now," she said.

"There's no one that can help you now. Only me. Allow me to help you."

"Please, just let me go."

Alphonso simply chuckled.

"I'll call the police," Esparanza declared, quite boldly.

"Please, allow me," Alphonso replied. He pulled out a flip cell phone. He spoke into the phone in a monotone voice, "Dial. Police." After a moment, someone answered.

"Richardson, I need you and Frasier to provide some assistance, please," said Alphonso.

Within minutes, an APD police car pulled up, and Officers Steve Richardson and Sam Frasier joined Alphonso and Esparanza in the office. Alphonso continued to harass Esparanza, trying to force her to admit her alleged police ties.

"I'm not a narc!" she screamed. "Stop this!"

Officer Richardson pulled out a bag of cocaine and wasn't shy in the least about doing so. Alphonso took some from the bag, placed some on a mirror, cut it into four lines, and snorted one whole line.

"Nice job, boss," said Richardson. Alphonso smiled and the officers laughed. "I bet she can take a line just as good as you, eh, boss?"

"Let's see," said Alphonso. He slid the mirror with the lines of cocaine toward Esparanza, and stated in a tone of voice that obviously wasn't going to be negotiable, "Do one for me."

"No," said Esparanza.

Alphonso pulled out a gun from under his coat and put it to Esparanza's head. "You do one of those lines now, or I blow your fucking head off. How's that?"

It was obvious to Esparanza now that Alphonso wasn't "right." He had to have been high to start with, long before she had ventured into his office. And she knew there would be no reasoning with him.

He had *snapped*.

Looking down at the table, Esparanza took the hard plastic straw and clumsily snorted a line. The men laughed as Richardson snapped a photo of her taking it in, another piece of blackmail to add to the stack.

Esparanza reeled back in her chair. Her eyes began to water. Her nose became very sore. Her mind began to spin. She closed her eyes to the maniacal laughter, anger and rage growing within her. Her heart began to race.

She thought of George and the happiness he brought her.

She thought of their wedding plans and how beautiful it would be. She thought of last night and how disappointing the sex was. Normally it was mind blowing, yet last night it was uninspired. It was really sad at this point as she thought that might have been the last moment of passion in this life.

She hoped it wasn't so.

The laughter and cruel banter continued as Esparanza thought of her family: her mother, her father, so far away, so far away. The smiles her little brother gave her, the laughs she shared with her sister, the hope she had for her older brother. Her mind began to focus, focus on the laughter, the derision, the debasement of her standards initiated by the forced drug use. The peace her loved ones gave to her racing heart began to be replaced by the rage in her soul that was growing as the chatter and giggles continued.

It had reached a boiling point.

She picked one of her many choices. Perhaps there were better options, perhaps not, but this was her first time being bullied.

And she didn't like it.

Richardson brought his face down toward the cocaine-lined mirror, the mirror that was within Esparanza's reach. Frasier had just withdrawn his nose and, sitting next to Esparanza, closed his eyes and allowed the drug to consume his mind. Alphonso's back was turned. He had put the gun away and was standing by a small bar at the far end of the table preparing a cocktail.

A gin and Sprite.

Richardson put the small plastic pipe to his nose and snorted a line. As the first grains of powder flew into his body, Esparanza brought her right hand down hard against the back of Richardson's head, like a hammer striking a nail. With the rage she initiated the strike with, it was more like Thor smiting a mythical foe with his sacred hammer. The pipe, congested with powder, lodged itself into Richardson's nasal cavity, cracking bones and tearing cartilage. His face smashed through the mirror, breaking the reflective plate, splitting shards of glass into Richardson's face and eyes. He clasped his hands over his nose, blood spitting from between his fingers, as he ran around the room screaming, "Crazy bitch! Crazy bitch!"

Frasier, surprised at the screaming, woke up from his stupor and saw Richardson's bloody face print on the table. Before he could react, Frasier's eyes caught sight of the back of a chair swinging toward his face. It landed square on his nose and jaw, crushing his nose and shoving his jawbone toward his spine, hitting the nerves and dislocating the jaw in the process. The concussive force put Frasier out.

As Esparanza threw the chair down, a solid blow to the back of her head brought her to her knees. Her hands moved toward the open wound on the back of her head as another blow sent her to the floor, her mind in a daze.

Coming back to the world after a second of darkness, Esparanza looked up and saw Alphonso standing over her, gun pointed at her face.

"All you had to do was *take it*. All you had to do was be cool. But you fucking bitch, I knew you were a cop."

Alphonso pulled the trigger just as Esparanza began to cry.

But there was a moment of hesitation. No fire. No bullet.

Alphonso had forgotten to take the safety off. Realizing this, Esparanza jumped to her feet, tears flying from her face, her mind still dizzy. As Alphonso released the safety, Esparanza knocked his gun away with one hand and gouged his right eye with the other. There was a wet *plop* sound as she pulled her thumb out, gross white fluid bursting from the socket and dripping from her finger. Alphonso screamed and covered his eye. Esparanza rushed to the door, stumbling once or twice from dizziness. She desperately reached out for the doorknob.

Surprisingly, she felt the sharp pain *first*.

Then she heard the blast.

As she lay there dying, she wondered why it wasn't the other way around.

George never knew the real story—never knew her suffering and pain in her final moments. He only knew she was gone and he didn't know why. She remained a ghostly phantasm that teased him in his dreams and visited his memories daily.

A memory locked forever in that gold crucifix necklace.

It was her gift.

It was her memory.

He had to get it back.

# Chapter 5

The road to Branton Junior High was not as serene as George remembered it being just days before. He passed two cars that had collided and caught on fire in the middle of the road. Their remains were two hulking shells of the vehicles they used to be, silent sentries on the road to Branton.

Farther past the wreck another car stood silent, stuck face-first in a ditch on the right side of the road. The back window was smashed and bloody. The carcass of what seemed to be a human hung out the back. Seemed to be, that is, as most of the flesh and limbs had been torn and mutilated some time before.

"Holy shit," George uttered. "*Holy shit.*"

A wave of uneasiness washed over George as he gazed at the carcass. This was real, this was very real. George stopped the Cavalier in the middle of the road and put the parking brake on. He looked ahead and in the rearview mirror. Ahead he could see the silhouette of the school on the horizon. Several clouds of smoke rose from fires in the far distance. Behind him, the two black sentinels stood where he had passed them, never to be driven again.

George realized he was all alone. No students driving from school. No cop waiting in a speed trap at the top of the hill; Just George and his vehicle in the middle of a fire-scorched and blood-stained stretch of road.

Leaving the vehicle running, George pulled his gun from his backpack and walked toward the vehicle in the ditch. The wind blew a bit and the aroma of rot caught his nose. He stopped in his tracks, gagging, and covered his nose with his shirt. Buzzards circled above.

George moved closer.

Approaching the driver's-side door, he noticed all the windows were smashed and bloody. He wondered, *What the fuck?* Looking into the back seat, George noticed the bottom portion of the rotting carrion had also been ripped apart. The shoes of what appeared to be a male were almost immaculate, the legs tangled in a buckled backseat belt.

*Strange sights for strange times,* he thought.

Peering through the broken driver seat window, George saw blood still dripping from the shattered passenger window. The smell was now penetrating his shirt and straight into his nose. A buzzard landed on the ground on the passenger side, just out of George's view.

George looked into the front seat area. Here was the usual. Old cups from a cheap corporate taco joint in the cup holders. They still had the plastic lid and straw in them. A dashboard Jesus covered in blood. The CDs were also speckled with the same genetic material that was caked on the dashboard Jesus.

Near the passenger seat on the floorboard, George noticed a plastic bag that seemed to be filled with stuff. Opening the door, he eased into the seat, taking care to avoid the blood, and reached for the bag. He grabbed it and stepped out of the vehicle.

Inside the bag were five bottles of water and five energy bars. All were untainted by the blood splattered in the car. The bag wasn't so lucky, though. Figuring the trip to investigate at least provided some free nourishment, George complimented himself.

*Good call, man, good call.*

The wind shifted again and a new smell of rotted flesh crept into George's nose. He pulled himself away from the vehicle as another buzzard descended near the ground by the passenger side door. George began to move back toward the Cavalier, but angled his walk to see what was attracting the buzzards.

Though he had an idea what it was, it still scared him when the body came into view. Just like the one coming out the back of the vehicle: torn, bloody, and lost forever. Buzzards were picking away at what was left. The remnants of long hair provided a clue that it must have been female.

The cold chill of viewing the body made George stride a little faster back to the Cavalier. The moans heard nearby also made the short trip a little more urgent.

George got in his car and locked the doors. He switched the air conditioner to high. He gazed past the ditched car and into the brush behind it, waiting to see if the moans had a face. As he waited, George looked at the wrecked and bloody car again and tried to make sense as to what happened.

*Ran off the road . . . by zombies? Surrounded and scared . . . passenger hurt? Stayed in car because they were scared . . . Creatures smash windows, pull out passenger from window . . . Driver tries to escape out the back . . . gets stuck in the seat belt . . . mauled . . . I guess staying in a parked car was not such a good idea . . .*

Concentrating on the field by the crash, George never expected the rotten hands and tattered face of a zombie to slam against his driver side window like they did. A loud yelp flew from George's mouth as he took the parking brake off and shifted to first gear. The creature struck at the window with its fists, creating an urgency that caused George to pull off the clutch a moment too soon.

He missed the gear.

The car stalled as the monster tried to open the door by yanking at the handle. Taking a breath, George turned the key in the ignition again, firing the engine, and efficiently shifted to first. The creature ambled along the side of the Cavalier, striking at the window as the car picked up speed. Two creatures finally emerged from the brush by the wreck, too late to cause George any harm.

Shifting to second, the back wheel of the car clipped the ankle of the zombie in pursuit, tearing the monster's Achilles heel, forcing its leg to become parallel with its foot as the wheel continued the forward motion. George was bumped in his seat a bit, as if he had hit a speed bump too fast. The force of the crushing movement caused the monster to fall forward, twisting its free leg awkwardly under its torso, which was falling forward, tearing the hamstring away from the bone, its face smacking against the pavement. Like rubbing salt in the wound, the same back wheel that crushed its foot proceeded to smash its hand as the Cavalier and George moved forward toward Branton Junior High.

George made several passes by the school along the street in front. There were quite a number of zombies wandering around the school, but none in a concentrated group. Some noticed his vehicle and some made an attempt to chase it from a distance. But they were no immediate threat, and most stopped their pursuit as the car moved farther away.

George decided it might be best to park behind a community real estate sign and dash over to the school, taking cover when needed. His plan, since he forgot the keys, was to find a way onto the roof to keep the journey relatively safe. He figured he could then break one of the many skylights, jump down, and walk to the classroom. Driving up to the school would attract too much attention and—recalling the car in the ditch—it might be a bit of a struggle to get out alive if a large group decided to bum rush the Cavalier. The window was obviously able to withstand one pile of deadshit banging away at it, but three or four doing the same would probably result in something similar to the ditch situation.

The group around the school wasn't all that large, at least by the naked eye. Most were scattered around the sides. And right now, there weren't so many in the front.

The time to make a run was now.

George turned off the ignition, put the parking brake on, and bowed his head in prayer. The Lord's Prayer. A Hail Mary. A personal request that he be safe and swift. A silent tribute to Esparanza, a quiet wish for his family's safety—the same family he started this journey down the road for.

The sign of the cross.

"Amen."

Looking out the window to check if the coast was clear, George exited the vehicle, closed the door and quietly began his mission as the five o'clock April sun bathed Branton and the surrounding area in a warm wash of light.

# Chapter 6

The dash across the street was swifter than expected as he positioned himself behind a tree, yards away from the school. Behind him, George noticed nothing peculiar by his car and the brush beyond it. Peering behind the tree toward the school, he saw the zombies were shambling around. It seemed like they hadn't noticed him.

In front of the school there was a covered walkway supported by brick columns. They were too high to jump straight up to, George reasoned, but if he angled a jump from one of those brick pillars, reaching the roof could very well be possible.

George prowled to a red car in the parking lot for a closer look at the angle. Crouching behind the car, George checked all sides. He hadn't been noticed by the walking corpses.

Not yet, at least.

Taking a deep breath, George sprinted across the bus lane in front of the school. Focusing on the pillar, George slowed his stride and leapt toward it.

Perhaps it was the speed, or maybe the shoes, but the

first flight from the pole to the edge of the roof fell short and George crashed on the pavement of the walkway with a highly audible, "Oooof!"

A zombie a short distance away, who had been meandering meaninglessly in front of a window, turned his head at the noise and watched George stand up. It then began to stumble toward George, moaning in a relatively loud fashion.

George turned and saw the zombie walking his way. It was yards away, but at the clip it was advancing, George would have only a few moments to get the jump right. The zombie let out another wail. George began his second attempt.

Another zombie several yards away in the opposite direction heard the first zombie's wail, turned, and saw George's second attempt fail. It shambled toward him, releasing a hissing groan.

George made a third attempt. It failed.

The two zombies crept closer, their cries attracting more attention.

Fourth attempt, failed. Fifth. Failed.

"Fuck!"

In desperation, George reached for his gun, not caring that the blasts would attract more attention.

Fortunately, he wouldn't have to worry about that because the gun wasn't there.

"FUCK!"

He realized then that he had left the gun in the car. In his obsession not to be seen, taking the gun off the passenger seat had completely slipped his mind.

*So fucking stupid . . .*

The zombies were yards away, but would be on him in seconds. He had a choice. Running to the car would only draw them to him, and George had no way of knowing if the path back to his car was clear now. Thinking about how he would be tailed, perhaps from all sides if he ran to the vehicle now, he pictured the car he saw in the ditch earlier.

That gave him the answer as to what he needed to do.

"If at first you don't succeed," George mouthed as he jumped toward the pillar.

His right foot planted, his knee bent. He pushed himself off the concrete post and grabbed the roof, first with one hand, then the other. George pulled himself up as one of the creatures reached for his shoe. He felt fingertips brush his ankle as he pulled himself all the way up.

He made it.

The roof was surprisingly hot. The rocks spread across the tar on the roof were uncomfortable to sit and place his hands on, so he stood. He could hear and see zombies gathering below. Taking a deep breath, George closed his eyes and made the sign of the cross in appreciation.

*Safe and swift.*

He crept across the rooftop in the direction of the room he taught, keeping out of view of the zombies below.

A gunshot fired in the distance. Smoke continued to billow into the sky from a neighborhood several miles away. What could have been a scream echoed from an unknown position far away.

George wondered how everything seemed to be falling

apart in just a matter of days. Several days earlier he was entering grades for the end of the semester. Now he was running for his life. It was crazy how things came unraveled so fast.

George walked toward one of several skylights. This one was closest to his room. However, before he had a chance to smash it a thought crossed his mind.

*How the hell are you going to unlock your door, genius?!*

He hesitated. Plan B was now shot, especially considering that there might be monsters inside. The glass shattering would surely gather a crowd. He came up with another solution.

Nearing the edge of the main building, George scanned the grassy courtyard area behind the school. A practice football field was in the distance. Green grass and dandelions, as well as some weeds, decorated the spot.

Several zombies crept around the area. George counted at least five in the vicinity, with one solitary creature standing in the middle of the football field, facing away from the school. Three of the five were an immediate threat. They shuffled around below him, by his classroom, near the window he planned to break through to enter the building. The zombies that were in the vicinity were far enough for George to take a chance, but too close to risk jumping down and smashing the window.

A distraction was in order. George figured these creatures were relatively smart, smart enough to follow a sound they might consider lunch, like a dog responding to a dinnertime bell. It was the oldest trick in the book, but George figured it should work.

He picked up a rock from the roof and tossed it in the corner of the building.

The rock clapped against the white brick wall of the school, like a hand slapping flesh. It echoed across the building.

All five zombies turned their heads and looked toward the location of the rock clap.

George held his breath for a moment.

All five zombies then turned their heads and looked toward George on the roof.

"Fuckin' shit, man," groaned George as the zombies approached his position.

Which also meant the window he planned to break through.

Which also would mean the end of plan C.

George climbed to the edge of the rocky roof quickly, ignoring the pain the rocks caused his forearms and elbows.

Clumsily hanging from the roof, the hot tar and rocks biting his fingers, George fell to the ground, square on his back. The wind rushed out of his lungs for a moment, stunning him for several seconds. The zombies approached, slow but steady, emanating a bizarre gurgling vocalization.

Gasping air back into his lungs, George scrambled to his feet. He removed his red flannel and wrapped it around his fist. With the zombies drawing ever nearer, George caught a whiff of their collective funk as he punched in the glass window. After gagging, he cleared the glass from the window sill just enough to crawl through.

Before he could get completely through however, one of the creatures made it to him, grabbing him by the shoulders and trying to pull him back outside. George swiped the dead hands away, then ducked to his right, gaining momentum, and sent a hammer fist to the creature's cods. It stumbled a bit, nearly regaining its balance before George pushed it down to the ground. Gagging again at the stench, he sprinted away toward the field. The quarters were getting a little tight and he needed a moment to regain his composure. He put his flannel back on, brushing off the stray bits of glass.

Creating a bit of distance between himself and the creatures, George looked to the ground for a stone. Though the zombie on the field was closer by a few yards, the other four near the window were the real issue that needed to be addressed. They all worked their way toward George, also therefore moving away from the now open window. Clearly, the ghouls could not formulate plans. Not one considered standing guard by the open window, George's obvious destination.

George saw a large stone in the ground, but it was stuck deep in the dirt. A brief attempt to remove it was futile. Rocks were useless—and if the previous rock usage was any indication—out of the question.

The zombies were closing in. Though George had an advantage in speed and agility, he still wanted a greater edge. Situating himself in the center of the advancing monsters, George stepped in a mud puddle near a leaking water sprinkler. It gave him an idea as the zombies almost encircled him, mere yards away.

Taking a large glob of mud in his right hand, George executed an unschooled front kick to the zombie from the field, delivering the boot square to the stomach. The creature collapsed from the blow, but not before regurgitating a gruesome black and red concoction of flesh, blood, and bile. George ignored some of the mess that stained his pants and, crouching down, he allowed the advance to continue.

When the lead zombie got close enough, George feinted left, drawing the creature in that direction, then he pounced downward, grabbing the creature by the cuff of its pants and yanked it upward with all his might, causing the monster to perform an impromptu split, effectively knocking it to the ground. George maneuvered himself in line with the window, the mud dripping from his right hand. His plan was to smack one of the creatures in the face with the mud, blinding it temporarily, giving him a shot at the window. He didn't need to get them all, just the one closest to the window. He saw an opening and took it.

Knocking away the hands of the two zombies closest to him, George rushed the one closest to the window and pied him perfectly in the face. Disoriented, the zombie was then shoved by George into the remaining two, knocking one to the ground and knocking the other off balance. While the other two were still trying to pick themselves off the ground (the one kicked in the stomach was still regurgitating filth and the one that did the split could not get off the ground, probably due to a torn hamstring) it gave George plenty of time to dash to the window, climb up, and enter his classroom.

He couldn't help but grin at the way he had handled himself.

*Safe and swift.*

Walking toward his desk, George angled to his computer. Below the plastic figure of Super Mario that stood glued on top of the monitor dangled the gold crucifix. Closing his eyes, George recited a silent prayer to himself, gave the sign of the cross, and gently took the crucifix into his hand. After gazing at it for a moment, he hooked the memento around his neck.

He had it.

Moments after securing the necklace, the zombie that had lost its balance appeared in the window and was attempting to climb in. Without hesitation, George yanked the computer monitor off the desk, cords dangling, and hurled the huge cathode ray tube generator toward the creature, smashing it over its head. Not much else was needed. It quivered and stopped moving, little plastic bits of casing stuck in its head like shrapnel.

Necklace secured, it was time to get out. Nightfall was coming and who knew what 35 South would be like. The wails from the fracas would likely attract more zombies to the area.

It was indeed time to go.

George was at heart a sentimental person, moved by movies, emotional for songs, sad at goodbyes.

Today was different.

When the world was relatively predictable, and butterflies flew from daisy to daisy, sentimentality could be a choice for the romantic. And George *was* a romantic.

But the world was now a place turned on its ear, a place of fear, of terror, of a true vast unknown. It could be argued that the past was just the same, but all would certainly agree that today and tomorrow would be filled with fear, terror, and the unknown. The course of humankind was seemingly heading in a new direction. Life was being measured in seconds, not years. As George saw for himself more than once in the most eventful day of his life, mere seconds meant the difference between life and death and between friends and family. Yesterday, sentimentality was a virtue.

Today it was a liability.

Literally ignoring his classroom and the memories made within and without its walls, George strode to the door, clapping his hands together to flick the mud off. Opening the door without a bye your leave or even a glance back in, something he would never consider doing several days before, knowing it was the last time he'd be in there, George left his classroom, closing the door behind him.

Outside, behind the feet of the ghoul stuck in the window, the figure of Super Mario lost itself in the dirt, rock, and grass behind Branton Junior High.

# Chapter 7

**W**alking out of the faculty restroom, George wiped his wet hands dry on his blue jeans. The mud was no problem to get off, though it left the sink a bit dirty. The real problem now was getting back to his vehicle.

Dashing through the hallway of Branton Junior High, with the lockers a blue blur in his peripheral vision, George thought he heard a scream. For a moment, he flinched and stopped in his tracks. Zombies? He looked back down the 200 hallway and saw that his classroom door was still closed. But sure enough, another scream emanated from the 300 hallway. Having stopped at the crossroads between the 200 and 300 hallway, George had an idea where the screams were coming from.

*Why the heck should I risk going to the 300 past all the windows?* George contemplated.

The hallway to the 300 hall was filled with windows to the outside. He knew that if any of the zombies outside the school were to see him run past the windows, they would surely try to break through them. At the moment, the hall-ways and the school were apparently secure, with only a few zombies still outside, though not necessarily threatening the building. Except, perhaps, at the window he entered through.

George thought about the creatures outside. They could have been *parents*—parents waiting to pick up their kids. Another thought crossed his mind. How long had they been waiting? How long are they *going to wait* for children who will never arrive? Then a smile came across his face. He chuckled as he realized that he may well have beat down some parents, something he dreamt of a lot of times dur-ing parent/teacher conferences. Surely somewhere, George thought, a teacher was smiling.

But before he could continue his parent ass–kicking daydream, the scream was heard again from the 300 as well as a clear cry for help. George recognized the voice as Keri Lawrence, one of the eighth-grade Language Arts teachers.

He breathed, "Goddammit."

As much as he just wanted to run, he couldn't let one of his friends be eaten alive, or whatever was happening to her.

Taking a deep breath, George bolted down the hallway to the 300 hallway. When he got to the windows he hit the floor, and, as swiftly as he could, crawled his way past the glass. It didn't take him as long as he thought, and he bolted around the corner into the 300 hallway.

He knew exactly where Lawrence's class was. And sure enough, the door was open.

*But what the hell am I going to do?* he thought, *I don't have any weapons.*

He continued to sprint toward the door, dreading that there might be too many ghouls to face unarmed. When he reached the doorway, he was somewhat relieved to see that there were only two. Keri was crouched in the corner of the room with a Language Arts book in hand. She had apparently held her own, keeping the two advancing cadavers at bay, but she was looking exhausted.

The light blue room was lined with inspirational posters. Crap like *You can do it!* and *The Future is in your hands* and *Respect is earned, not given.* The walking cadavers had knocked over several desks and torn several posters off the wall. One of the torn pictures showed a small kitten hanging from a rope, the caption reading, *Don't give up now!*

Taking another heavy Language Arts book in hand, George darted toward the nearest zombie, running down an aisle of desks, and clobbered it with the flat side across the skull. It wasn't very graceful, but it worked. The zombie collapsed.

Then, as Keri noticed George, in a tone of voice that sounded relieved and at the same time shocked at just who her rescuer was, she gasped, "Mister Zaragosa?!"

As the first zombie fell, stunned, the second zombie turned toward George. Perhaps it was the particularly bad stench of this one, or maybe it was seeing all the maggots crawling in and out of its nostrils, but this time George threw up on the floor. He couldn't help it. Recovering, he drew a deep breath and held it, waited for the creature to amble closer, then cracked it in the nose, breaking its face. The creature slowly fell to the floor, but not before George smacked it twice more on the head for good measure.

Keri Lawrence had already begun to stomp the first zombie in the back of the head and neck with her knee-high heeled boots until it stopped moving. The rancid odor had a disgusting effect on her nervous system. After her fifth boot stomp, with the flesh and blood of the cadaver moistening the bottom of her light brown boot, the stench of decay overtook her senses and she felt like vomiting on the now unmoving corpse. She ran to get some fresh air outside the classroom.

George, trying to finish the job on his adversary, picked up a desk and dropped it with authority on the back of the head and neck of the second beast. The sound of bone breaking and blood splattering was heard as George stumbled away from the reeking dead body. He heard Keri gag outside, and dashed outside to join her.

When he exited the room, she was leaning against a locker. Her head dipped down as if in prayer, but clearly to make room for anything that might fly out of her mouth. She gagged one more time as George reached her. He stood beside here, waving his hand in the air to get some fresh air circulating.

"I'm all right. I'm all right," she insisted. "Just give me a second."

George stepped back. Keri was wearing a simple white top, with a light skirt made for summertime. High-heeled boots complemented her legs. Had it been any other situation, George might have been turned on. But listening to Keri's gagging and seeing the trail of zombie gore tracked from her room to the locker by her boot took away from the moment.

The gore on the floor took George away for a moment. He had seen more blood and death in one day than in his entire life, from the moment he grappled with the first creature that morning, to running over the cops in Austin to escape from the city. Then there were the remains of the people in the car just about a mile away from the school who became a meal for vultures. And now, in a classroom, a safe haven in the old world, George had once again unleashed a savage beating on one more ghoul, the remnant of a human being.

Sure, movies and TV had its fill of violence. But it was somehow different in real life. While the movies made a great effort catching the sounds and visual effects of a savage beating or other physical abuse, TV or film could never provide the element of scent. The sense provided a whole new element to violence, and George and Keri experienced it firsthand today, like people around the world in the past few days.

George was drifting. Even Keri was becoming a blur, like a ghost.

This savagery, this new necessity to destroy the apparent remnants of a human being on the streets and neighborhoods of the United States of America was a cruel edict by an unpredictable universe. Nations around the world, perhaps, had been exposed to this kind of savagery. Fighting each other, other tribes, other people in streets, marketplaces, might be commonplace. Surviving or experiencing a car bombing, or shootouts, or riots against a tyrannical government were experiences not common to the American lifestyle. Americans preferred their violence on a film screen or in the privacy of their own homes. Kids played video games where they blasted people with modern weapons after finishing their homework. And then they could lie down and go to sleep in complete safety.

But now, America was in survival mode. Apart from the military, no American was prepared for the kind of extreme violence needed to survive, to protect their families, to save their friends. This was a new world, with new necessities uncommon to the middle-American experience. And though George was a quick study, allowing that most primitive side of his humanity to surface, it was still taking a psychic toll.

George was so lost mentally, in a mild catatonic state, that he barely noticed Keri yanking him away from the room, dashing down the hall he had run up to save her.

Night wrapped its black pall over the small town of Koehl and the after hours lights of the school illuminated areas of darkness around Branton Junior High. It was a good thing too, because the sparkle of the stars were playing hide and seek in the clouds.

George and Keri held each other, legs and arms comfortably entangled, as they lay together on a bed in the nurse's office. Several candles found around the office illuminated the room. Flickering reflections of flame licked the walls and massaged their bodies.

They were safe for the moment.

Laying together, Keri looked to George. "George, are you OK?"

George was finally coming out of his semi-trance.

Perhaps it was the candles, or the relaxation. Perhaps it was just the opportunity to lay down and relax with Keri. The peace of the moment drawing him back to the real world, away from his psychic malaise.

An awkward silence ensued. They rested for a moment in silence. No words were spoken. They both gazed into the quiet light of the flickering flames dancing across the walls.

Keri looked at George, who was still staring blankly at the ceiling. She gently kissed his cheek and tightened her embrace. George returned the loving hug. A tear formed in his eye.

"It's so weird sometimes," George began. "Life, you know. I came here to get this." He lifted the gold crucifix dangling from his neck. "Esparanza gave it to me. I just had to have it before I went home." He paused. Keri rested her head on his chest.

"So I get it, fight to get it," George continued, "and then I end up here with you. Ironic, isn't it?"

Keri nodded. She knew the Esparanza story and sympathized with George.

"I came here to secure Esparanza's memory," George went on. "The memory of the woman I love and who loved me like no other. Yet I spend the remainder of the same day here with you."

"What's wrong with that?" asked Keri.

"What do you mean?"

"Well, what's wrong with being together?' We're friends, right?"

"Right."

"As a friend, you care about me, right? I care about you."

"Well, yeah."

"I obviously felt the same way you did. You didn't force me to do anything."

*What the fuck is she talking about?* thought George to himself. Had they had sex? The horror of the day had affected his reality, his consciousness.

Keri continued. "I wanted to. I didn't say no. To anything and everything we did today. It's not hypocritical to want comfort when and where you can get it." She paused and smiled. "And I am certainly glad we did. Wow!"

George tried to remember, and had a vague recollection of intimacy. He relaxed in solemn contemplation of his confusion. "I'm just not sure why I'm here anymore."

Keri was becoming confused, but tried to make sense of it all by continuing her train of thought, thinking he was referencing his love of Esparanza. "It's all right to feel that way. You loved her. Or should I say, you *still* love her. There's nothing wrong with that. I have those feelings for other people I dated throughout my life. But they're all gone now, George. Far away from here. A different time, a different place. The love that we have for them, and our family, our friends, will always be in our hearts. And that's the truth. They will *always* be in our hearts."

George closed his eyes. Keri was an eloquent speaker, and her words were very comforting. He listened more intently, inching his way back to reality.

She continued, "That's the past, George. It's gone. It doesn't exist anymore. All we have is now. And with the way the world is going, we need to learn that. All we have is now. A chance to share this passion that we've always had. A chance to love each other. A chance to be human. To love, to fear, to care. That's being human. Look at the world around us. There's never been a more important moment to be here, to be now, to be human, than in this moment." She stared blankly at the wall, wondering silently if she was making any sense at all, adding, "We have to. We *have* to."

They sat in silence for a few moments, meditating.

Keri was overcome with a slight sense of jealousy. They had, indeed, shared an intimate moment together, yet George still talked about his love for his dead fiancée. She spoke, "You came all this way for her, for her gift. You risked great danger to be here today, all to honor her memory. You did that. Hell, you did more for her now than most men do for their lovers and wives when they're alive. That's special. That's very special!"

They sat again in silence, contemplating the comments.

George thought about the horrors his day had presented yet again. Leaving the apartment, the news, I-35, killing the cops, fighting the zombies, the car in the ditch.

Keri put her hand on George's cheek and gazed into his eyes. She sensed his confusion, his distance. She tried to reel him in, to comfort him. "You're very special, George. Esparanza was lucky to have a fiancée as sweet as you, and I'm so glad I have a friend like you. Please George, be here, be *now*. This moment together, to support each other, to care for each other, to love each other, might be all we have left."

*She's right*, thought George. All that lay ahead of the two was unknown. A legitimate threat would loom over their lives when they left the building, perhaps forever. George knew the importance of life, especially after today.

He also knew the importance of love. It was love for his family that sent him on his journey down the road. It was love for Esparanza that brought him here. And it was love for the beauty in Keri's heart, the heart that was trying to keep his mind in one piece, that brought George's lips to hers once again.

"Thank you, Keri. Thank you."

After a moment, they relaxed. As they repositioned themselves for sleep, George asked a question.

"Keri?"

"Yeah?"

"What in the world were you doing here anyway?"

"Entering grades. I guess I was in denial, huh?"

"No shit you were in denial."

After taking time to find a comfortable spot in and around each other, they shared a final kiss and drifted off to sleep.

# Chapter 8

The back roads into San Marcos looked similar to the road to Branton. Crashes, carnage, and corpses littered the path of the Cavalier. In several instances, zombies waddled from a wreck or the brush to try and take the vehicle and its passenger. But the Cavalier's speed always kept it from any real danger. George knew things were different in San Marcos than they were in Koehl. The number of dead walking the roads was one indication, the smoke flowing into the sky from the city was another.

The morning had started pleasantly enough. George and Keri got their clothes and gear together, then had one last hurrah, so to speak, on the bed in the nurses office before making their way to their respective vehicles. It was a mad dash to Keri's car, and a brief scuffle with the undead brought some tension to the moment. But their swiftness to the vehicle checked any aggression toward the two.

Keri wanted to head back to Austin. She knew that it might be a mess by now, and the roads might be peppered with monsters if George's stories were any measure of truth.

She wanted to try to contact her family in Houston if the phones still worked before holing herself up in her apartment, or maybe with some friends. Like George, she wasn't much for the FEMA camp idea, and certainly didn't trust any member of Homeland Security.

George wanted to take a back road through San Marcos, New Braunfels, and into San Antonio to get to San Uvalde.

With a last kiss, they said goodbye before a crowd could gather, driving off in different directions.

George hit the back roads to get to San Marcos. On the drive, he ejected his tape and put on the radio station. The first station had an announcement. He tuned to another, which was playing the same announcement. A third, the same.

*I guess FEMA has completely taken over the airwaves.*

On his fifth try, George found a pirate radio station. He set it to his dial. The song was "My Eyes Adored You"— One of George's favorites. He listened to the song to the end, then changed it when they started playing Clay Aiken.

On his seventh try he found another. He set it to the dial. This station was a stark contrast to the FEMA controlled stations. This one was actually encouraging people to hole up in their homes or someplace with their family and friends and to get as many weapons, guns, and as much ammunition as possible. It also instructed how to find food and how to purify water.

*Sweet*, thought George.

The anti-takeover station continued to give information as George hit 35. It was a mess, an out-and-out demolition derby with other drivers just to get to where he was now, a back road entering San Marcos from the east. No real damage was sustained to the black Cavalier apart from some scrapes and bumps to the exterior.

And now, this road. Dead walking. Cars in flames. Flesh being eaten. A sign of the times.

A light flashed on the Cavalier's dashboard. Gas low.

Fortunately, there was a gas station just down the road.

Post Road. A line of trees loomed over the pavement and wreckage as George worked his way down it. It was a familiar road, taken by George and his friends when they traveled to and from Austin. It was a shortcut that took them straight back to their apartments, which were near the end of the road and away from the stop lights of San Marcos.

George crossed a bridge and drove past the trailer park near his old apartment. Well, what was left of the park. Most of it was in flames.

George passed two cemeteries on the way. The cemeteries were over a century old. He remembered where they were located and accelerated just a bit faster. He wondered why, though. Skeletons couldn't get up, could they? And with the way the dead were literally locked away in their coffins, it wasn't likely they could even get out.

He further wondered what exactly the undead needed to be able to walk again. All their flesh or just muscles or just a brain? Wouldn't the preservation process, the embalming, take away the facilities to live again? The brain remained connected to everything, even though the blood was drained away.

*So it's the brain*, he reasoned. *It must be the brain.*

Up ahead was the old apartments, Mossy Mount, which

brought back many fond memories for George. It was the unofficial party central of San Marcos, with weekly beer bashes commonplace. George's friends were usually the official sponsors of many of them. Twelve kegs was a crazy idea, but came to fruition under the advice and charisma of Edwin, one of George's wilder friends. He figured with the participation of just a few of the apartments outside of Little South Side (the area of the apartment complex they all lived in) then they could each have a keg or two a piece. Then, with the friend of a friend of a friend who hears word of the party, several hundred people would show up, increasing the craziness and raising the unruly reputation of Mossy Mount Apartments.

The wildest of the group of revelers would always be George's friends from the theatre department. Lots of alcohol, some pot, and cute girls all around. George let the pot users do their thing. His roommate, Robert, a grad student, usually entertained several times a night during a party in his room in their apartment.

But George liked the beer. The beer and the girls. One night, one of the flirty aspiring actresses offered to share her leg strength with George that she had gained through years of formal ballet training. She wrapped her legs around him and squeezed for several seconds. It hurt, but was cool. Very few girls did anything like that for George in his early days of college. Hell, even in high school. He was always kind of a dork, even though he knew everybody and got along with everyone.

For George, it wasn't that the girls weren't there or that he didn't have any opportunities. His chivalrous manners and schoolboy charm attracted the fancy of many a high school and college co-ed. Lots of kisses, some playful groping, and the occasional flash made college time and studying more interesting. But George would always hold back, convinced choosing chivalry over debauchery would help him find the dream girl who could satisfy him for the long term.

It almost did.

Since Esparanza's death, George's manufactured chastity was becoming negotiable. However, his chivalrous and true nature would not change. That was just the way he was. But when an invitation for intimacy presented itself, George would accept it—and in a chivalrous fashion—take it as far as it would go.

Hence the lustful encounter at the Junior High.

He would always love Esparanza, he knew, and even though there was a tinge of guilt after his encounters with other women after her death, it still made the pain of Esparanza's absence just a little less intense, even if only temporarily.

Past Mossy Mount and along the road was a train track. To his left, George passed the fiery remnants of a derailed cargo train. He could see in the clearing there were shadowy figures moving around the wreckage and some in the adjacent neighborhood. Deciding those figures probably weren't friendly, he accelerated ahead.

As he neared the gas station he noticed a large barrier in the middle of the road. A crude blockade of dumpsters, wrecked cars, couches, and mattresses stood between the Cavalier and the gas station. Several figures stood on and around the makeshift barrier. It didn't look too official, so

George slowed to a stop. He was close enough to scope it out, but far enough to drive away if needed.

Two figures approached the Cavalier. Both had rifles. They waved, holding the rifles in a non-aggressive manner. They seemed to be smiling, so George repositioned the vehicle to turn the other way and rolled down his window.

He called out, "Who are you guys?" as he stealthily put his gun in the back of his pants.

"Hello," one called back. He was a white guy in dirty overalls and a green t-shirt underneath, sporting an orange trucker hat.

"Hello," replied George, figuring they didn't hear him. "Who are you guys?"

"We're here to help, if you need it." They edged closer to the car. "My name's Jeff. That's—"

A shot rang out from the barricade. The two guys ducked. George almost went for his gun while ducking in the car, but realized it was in his defense. A zombie fell on the other side of the car, a large hole in the back of its head.

"Goddammit, Arnold, you asshole!" yelled Jeff's companion. "Use the megaphone and tell us you're firing!"

A loud sound of electric feedback was heard and Arnold replied from the barricade with an artificially projected, *"Sorry 'bout that!"*

Jeff moved by the Cavalier, his rifle over his shoulder. He leaned on the hood of the car. "As I was saying, I'm Jeff and that's Michael." Michael smiled and waved, pointing his rifle to the ground.

"I'm George."

They shook hands.

"*Clear!*" yelled Arnold from the barricade. All ducked, a shot rang out, another zombie fell.

"You in charge of the pumps now?" asked George.

"You got it," replied Jeff. "Always have been. You want some gas?"

"Sure do."

"Thirty bucks for a full tank, no questions asked."

George was a bit of a cheapskate. Thirty was double what he would usually pay, but a full tank would be plenty to get him back to San Uvalde and beyond. After a moment he replied, "You got a deal."

Jeff turned back to the barricade. "Open it up!"

George gassed up, paid Jeff the thirty dollars, and chatted it up with him and Michael inside the convenience store.

The little commune had a unique setup, reminiscent of a fort. The walls were dumpsters, various large objects, and an unusual amount of cars, all set up in a kind of half moon from the road where George entered, then running parallel to the train tracks all the way to the entrance of an elementary school across the street from the convenience store. Along the barrier were many men and women with guns. Every now and then a shot would be fired as a creature would find its way to the barrier and try to penetrate it.

Inside the elementary school were locals from surrounding neighborhoods. Figuring there was strength in numbers, people gathered their supplies and families in the school. Most everyone had a gun or some other form of weapon, as they knew some zombies still found ways to sneak in. Once shot in the head, those zombies were disposed of in the back of the school where they would be piled up and set on fire at the end of the day.

For the most part, the women and children were encouraged to stay in the elementary school. Older people were also part of the commune, and the ones that had a hard time helping outside were also encouraged to stay in the school.

George was sitting against the ice cream freezer under the front counter of the convenience store. Large boards covered the usually transparent windows. The store itself was a bit of a mess, but still had large quantities of supplies, and even more in the storage room in the back. It seemed like most of the mess was empty beer cans and bags of chips. There was stuff all over the floor, but Jeff seemed to want to keep it relatively organized. He sat in a chair near George as Michael stood looking out the door at the barricade.

Jeff was the proprietor of the store. His family and his buddies had joined him when the shit started hitting the fan. Most of his family and friends brought their own weapons.

"It was crazy," explained Jeff as they both ate a nuked hot dog and a bag of chips. "Two days ago was when it really started affecting people here, and attacks by those creatures began to happen all over town, especially on the college campus. All the college types that lived down the way hit the roads—*and the pumps*—pretty hard. Good thing the tanker truck came by the day before. Well, the same day, people decided they didn't have to pay for gas anymore."

"Fuckin' Betas," chimed in Michael as he handed George

and Jeff a Coke. "Spoiled rich-assed brats thought they could take what they wanted."

George understood so far. The Beta Alpha Chi fraternity house was down the road. The irony, of course, was that Michael was a Theta Epsilon Kappa, as his frat shirt revealed.

"Michael had brought some of his friends over to help me. See, he lived down the way at Mossy Mount and him and his friends were some of my best customers." He took a chomping bite from the hot dog and followed it with a swig of Coke.

"Jeff walked outside and put an 'Out of Gas' sign on the pumps. Most didn't give a damn, just wanted to get the fuck out. Some yelled shit from their cars. Fact was, there was a whole line of cars trying to get up the road and out of this place—to their hometowns, I guess."

Jeff jumped in. "But the fuckin' Betas took issue with the 'Out of Gas' sign. They gathered by the pumps."

"That's where my boys, the Thetas, jumped in," stated Michael with pride. "It was like those old school gang movies, with pipes and boards and shit. Like *West Side Story* without all the damn singing."

"It was a brawl, let me tell you," stated Jeff. "For about five minutes, it was a whirlwind of beatdown in the parking lot. But then things really got all messed up."

"No shit," stated Michael.

George took a swig of soda and ate a couple of chips as the story continued.

"While the brawl was heating up, it was looking good for

71

Michael's Thetas." Jeff finished his hot dog. "Three or four Betas were already calling it quits and licking their wounds near all the traffic on the road. Then it happened."

"A small wave of those fucking monsters—about ten or twelve—came out from the neighborhood across the tracks and started attacking the cars," said Michael, taking a seat on two unopened cases of malt liquor.

Jeff popped open a can of Old Milwaukee. "It was like watching a goddamn fucked-up Indy 500 of spooked cattle. The cars that were attacked hit the gas and started a car stampede. They all started trying to work themselves up the road, crashing and a-ramming each other. Some flipped into the ditch by the tracks, lots just wrecked. People started getting out of their cars and just started running."

"But those Betas got it worst. The deadfucks that made it past the cars attacked the poor bastards that were injured from the fight and tore into 'em." Jeff paused for a moment. Michael sat quietly, staring at the chocolate mints and spicy candy on the rack in front of him. He looked tempted. "Never seen anything so ugly in all my life. Blood everywhere. Those kids started screaming as those monsters . . ." Jeff paused again, swallowing hard, then continued, ". . . As those monsters bit into them. They tore whole chunks— just *whole chunks* out of those kids' necks. Their arms. And just blood . . . *everywhere.*"

Jeff stopped talking. He pulled out a pack of Lucky Strikes and took a mini lighter out from the display rack by the register. He lit the smoke, took a drag, exhaled.

"You know, those frat bastards might have been assholes, but even they didn't deserve what happened to them."

Michael wanted to say something—wanted to condone the slaughtering of the frat guys—but he held back and respectfully remained silent. George bummed a smoke, remembering the parking lot he just walked across. The pavement was stained a dark red, almost as thick as the motor oil and other automotive fluids staining every parking lot in Anytown, USA. He lit up the cigarette and took a drag.

Jeff finished the story. "When the screams were heard, the fighting stopped within seconds. The boys just stared at them, stared in this kind of shocked disbelief, some of them with blood dripping out of their noses and heads. It took one of the creatures lunging at them to wake them up. Most of the Betas just ran; ran away into the mess of cars. Some went to help their comrades. Not enough, though. I rounded up the remaining Thetas in here and brought my brothers and male family out with the guns. It was quite a sight. Cars wrecking and blowing up. Zombies everywhere. And those kids . . . goddamn *kids*."

Jeff continued, "My brother Frank told the family to open up on those frat guys *and* the monsters. Word had come saying that getting bit by one would turn you into one in hours—sometimes even *minutes*. They blew them all away. Probably did them a favor. I went back inside and joined the others. I couldn't take it." Jeff frowned. "You know, after the Gulf War, looking at all those dead kids, soldiers, the Highway to Hell, you think you've seen it all. You don't want to see that shit again. Never thought something like it would be at my front door, you know?"

Everyone was silent for a moment. Michael got up and put his hand on Jeff's shoulder. George looked out the open door of the grocery store. "I'm all right," Jeff told Michael. "I'm fine, man."

But it was obvious that he wasn't.

Jeff went on: "Anyway, with all that gunfire, we're sure as shit lucky this place didn't blow. They were out there for close to a half hour, just firing away. When they were done we took a break, made barriers with the wrecked cars, and secured the store and the elementary school next door with boards and stuff."

A shot was heard from outside. George winced, but Jeff and Michael remained unfazed.

"Since then, we got a little community-thing going. Lots of people found their way here yesterday. Lots from the surrounding neighborhoods, most getting run out of their houses by the beasts, some running away from the feds."

Michael commented, "Some of the people that came in said that FEMA had set up shop at the high school and college football fields and indoor basketball courts. Helluva place to feel safe, huh? Homeland Security started rounding people up yesterday, making them get ID tags, corralling them up in fenced-off areas. Lots of military and barbed wire. To *protect them*, they said."

Jeff jumped in, "Looks more like a prison camp than a refuge."

"Fuckin' A," agreed George. Familiar with the area, he knew the camp itself was just three blocks away, beyond the railroad tracks, in the same direction all the cars were headed.

"We got some escapees coming from the camp, too. Some bring food to share with the whole community. We're operating under the assumption that it's going to get better. That's why I'm still charging for stuff, food not so much as the gas. I do have a bit of charity."

Jeff took a final drag off the cigarette and smashed it under his foot. "Well, they're rounding people up, as I said. Don't know how long that will last, though. Whatever the hell's causing these monsters to attack hasn't wore off yet. By tomorrow, there might be more of them than us. And if that damn camp falls, who knows what will happen to us."

"Yeah, and it don't even have to fall from *outside*," Michael pointed out. "All it would take is one or two people dying unattended in that camp, waking back up, and starting to chomp on people to fuck that situation up—real quick."

George spent the day and part of the night at the camp based on Jeff's advice. He claimed the FEMA people didn't dare leave their camp at night looking for other people. His advice made sense. So George made some friends, played a game of chess with a ten-year-old (and lost) watched the FEMA camp at the stadium through binoculars, and rested. All in all, it was a fairly relaxing day, with the camp members keeping the hordes at bay behind the wreckage.

George planned to sleep through the night and leave at around five the next morning, just before the sun came up. Finding a cozy corner of a classroom, George drifted off to sleep.

After a few moments, he began to dream.

He was back in his Austin apartment, or so it felt. Esparanza was holding him in what felt like the old bed. The warmth of her love revisited his heart, and George smiled. Esparanza got up and walked out the door. George stood up and followed her, seeing a long dirt path filled with old trees. He took the path without hesitation. The trees burst into flames. He tried to put it out with a bucket of water, but the fire only got stronger. He was starting to catch on fire when Esparanza pulled him into the movie theater parking lot of San Uvalde. In flames, Esparanza pleaded with him, crying, "Kill him . . . Kill him . . . *Kill him.*"

"Who?" George asked. "Kill *who?*"

"Wake up and go!" she commanded.

An explosion—shaking the building and cracking the ceiling—rattled George from his sleep. Jeff was running into the room, an expression of fear on his face.

"If you're trying to get home, you'd better hoof it now! Those military fuckers from FEMA are attacking the place!"

Gunfire and explosions were erupting outside. The building shook again.

George's gear was still in his car by the gas station. He and Jeff ran through the halls among a large crowd of men, women, and children. Lots of yelling, lots of screaming, lots of crying. Another explosion punched a hole in the wall behind them. The force of the blast threw them to the ground, their ears ringing.

Four girls, two children, and a man weren't so lucky. Most ended up a red mess on the adjacent cracked wall. The others were in pieces.

The man's weapon, an AK-47, fell by Jeff. It looked functional.

More screams and crying children were heard as a series of rapid gunfire shots resonated across the breached hallway.

They were, indeed, under attack—a balls-out attack meant to crush them.

When George and Jeff exited the building, they finally got to see exactly what was going on. A large tank had shot a huge gap in the automotive barrier, and a small group of green camouflaged soldiers—in hi-tech gear and armed to the teeth—were storming the place, laying waste the valiant, yet untrained, survival community. A field of wholesale slaughter was forming in front of their eyes.

Through a loudspeaker, a booming voice was heard. "This is Homeland Security. We are here to help. Please lay down your weapons and follow us to safety at the FEMA center. You are not being attacked. Homeland Security is here to help. Repeating, you are not under attack."

From worse to even worse, the assault was opening up the community to the living dead, who were beginning to enter in increasing numbers in the trail of the soldiers.

Jeff yelled, "Some of the escapees warned they were going to do this, but I didn't think it would be this soon!" He passed the AK-47 to George. "I know you've got family to get to. There's a large group of us that's making a break for it." He pointed to his gas station where cars were already hauling ass out. The military didn't have as much man- or firepower at the end where George had entered, and it looked like a good escape route. "But you need to fuckin' go now!"

"What about you?"

"That's *my* gas station, friend."

"Bad ass," complimented George. Bullets ricocheted over their heads.

"Go!" yelled Jeff as he began firing toward the advancing column of digital gray.

George sprinted to his car.

"Homeland Security is here to help. You are not under attack."

Overhead, a helicopter began emptying its content of soldiers onto the roof of the elementary school. Explosions rocked the roof of the school as the black-clad and masked force entered the school. George knew there were only some women, children, and old men in the school.

*Those bastards*, he thought.

Gunfire, blasts, and screams shook George's eardrums as he raced to the car. Several soldiers were opening fire on some of the barrier men, smearing them across the cars and mattresses of the barricade near the exit. George hit the ground, pointed the barrel of the AK-47 at the soldiers, and pulled the trigger. Sparks erupted from the end of the gun and the butt-end rattled violently against George's shoulder. When he let his finger off the trigger he saw that the soldiers were down. But dead? He wasn't sure. Getting up off the ground in a hurry, George saw creatures coming through the barrier as well.

"Lay down your weapons and follow a member to the FEMA center at the stadium. We are here to help."

Several more vehicles hit the exit—and each other—on the way out as George unlocked his car, fired it up, and sped to the exit. George turned the corner just as a soldier came running in, colliding violently with the soldier's right leg and snapping it in two. The soldier discharged his weapon in agony, hitting some of his own men who were pushing back the barricade community.

Two helicopters were chasing down and firing on the vehicles that escaped past the feeble sandbags and machine gun nest set behind the back barricade, though two cars had been sacrificed to take it out. The group was so spread out that the helicopters were forced to be selective in their pursuit, meaning some were getting a clean break.

George was lucky.

Finding an old neighborhood several blocks away from the barricade and the FEMA camp, George pulled into an open garage of a house, turned off the lights, and cut the ignition, and sat out the search and destroy mission by the helicopters.

No creatures were in the vicinity, or at least in plain view.

George secured the house.

It was two o'clock in the morning.

George opened the fridge. There was a half empty case of beer inside. He busted one open, took a long swig, and tried to relax. Images of the battle that was the siege, and the massacre of the barricaded people, were haunting him. He took another swig of warm beer and had a seat on the living room couch. He threw a coffee table book across the room at a mirror, breaking the reflecting plate, angry at the useless massacre by the soldiers. The slaughter was taking a toll on George's soul. Another piece of his sacred spirit was bruised and beaten by the visions of death he had walked through. He didn't know all of the people, never got to know them. But he most certainly watched them die, the only moment of their lives shared with him. The only way he would remember them. Not for their accomplishments. Not for their failures, or even for their smiles or laughs. George would only know them for how bullets punched through their bodies, how the blood fell on their faces, or how a ghoul ripped them to pieces.

After an hour, George headed to the bedroom. He set some primitive alarms by all the doors and windows (empty beer can pyramids) and locked the door. After locating an alarm clock, he set it for five o'clock a.m., then laid on the bed and went to sleep.

The city of San Marcos seemed vacant, but not completely empty. Every now and then a creature would be in the road, or be exiting a building as George drove through downtown. The Cavalier was still too swift for them.

Trash and paper was everywhere. Some of the building fires had done their job, leaving the buildings as nothing more than a black memory.

The plan was to hit another back road, get to the New Braunfels loop, then make it to south 35 to San Antonio. He decided the city was big enough (one of the nation's mightiest metroplexes) that he would take his chances.

George drove slowly through town. Though it seemed deserted, he still drove carefully, as if a truck might barrel its way around a corner at any minute.

George entered the city plaza. Had it been a normal day he might have parked and entered one of the many bars encircling the plaza. There was certainly plenty of parking today.

A figure darted out of sight from a rooftop. George looked up, but not in time to make out what it was.

George slowed the Cavalier down at a four-way and shifted into neutral.

The view of the road to the right was obstructed by a smoldering building.

He looked to the left. Nothing there.

He looked straight ahead. It was wide open—not even a monster or wrecked car. That was a good thing, as the back road he wanted to reach was just ahead.

He looked to his right one more time.

A wooden bat smashed George's driver-side window. Glass flew toward his face, but he averted his head just in time to avoid getting cut.

Someone opened his door and yanked him from the car with a vicious heave. Two boys began to stomp at him and kick at his ribs.

They were Betas, whooping and hollering.

"Kick that spic's ass!" one yelled.

George surmised that there were probably four of them. One had a baseball bat. One was in the driver's seat of his Cavalier. They were obviously looters, a roving gang of thugs looking for anything that might help them survive.

"It's standard," said the driver, turning to bat boy. "Can anyone drive standard?" He popped the clutch, causing the car to stall. "Shit, what did I do?"

Bat boy was walking toward the two kicking at George.

"I got him," said bat boy.

"Oh, shit, a fuckin' machine gun," said the driver, looking in the passenger seat.

As bat boy moved closer to the two guys kicking George on the ground, it gave George the opportunity to pull his .38 from the back of his pants. He hurriedly flicked off the safety and aimed the gun at bat boy.

George gut shot him, then repeated the same on the two that were kicking him. The beating had sent him over the edge, chomping another piece out of his humanity like a hungry man eating a cheeseburger.

The guy in the car reached for the AK in the passenger seat. Before he could figure out how to take it off the safety, George yanked him by the hair out of the car, smashed his mouth with the butt of the .38, and shot him in the neck. The bullet severed the spine, bathing the other three in blood, the head barely holding on by a shred of flesh.

The driver was dead. His body began to shake in shock, nerves trying to figure out what the hell had happened.

George sent the fifth bullet in the chamber through bat boy's heart. The muscle exploded out his back, moistening the street below. The other two Betas, bleeding profusely, began to beg off.

*Cowards*, thought George. *Nothing but bullies and cowards.*

His father shared a pearl with him once about bullies. It was many years ago. George had to have been eight or nine.

On a sunny summer afternoon, while sitting with his father talking about school bullies, he had told George, "Mijo, bullies are really just cowards. You shouldn't be afraid of them. If you punch them right in the mouth or nose, they'll leave you alone. They only like to pick on the weak. Show them you're not, and they'll leave you alone."

George then hugged his dad.

"I love you, Mijo. Don't be afraid."

"I love you, too, Dad."

He remembered back in school how a couple of bullies had made his life miserable—taking his pens, teasing him, making him cry in front of his friends and girls he liked. No fun. George never avenged the wrongdoing by the bullies.

Then he thought, *These fuckers probably did the same thing to somebody, somewhere, making their lives miserable . . . Hurting them, embarrassing them.*

Two were bleeding and dead. Two were crying and begging for their own survival.

"Please, please don't hurt me."

"Please, don't!"

Those were the same words George would cry in his youth. That same pain came back for a second. The universe was balancing out an old score. A past wrong would be righted, maybe not for George, but for a few. The universe pushed George to help its balancing act.

Prepared to unleash a furious anger, George was stopped by a sound beyond the crying of the frat boys. It was clear. Unmistakable.

Somewhere close, the moans of the living dead were marching toward them.

George was ready to burst the frat boys' hearts with his gun, but he hesitated. Across the plaza, a large group of the undead were gathering and walking their way.

Swiftly, George removed the glass from the driver's-side seat and opened the glove compartment to get more bullets. He hovered over the weeping and dying Betas as he reloaded.

He shouted, "How's it feel now, huh?! C'mon, tell me! *How's it feel?!*"

"Please, don't hurt us! Please!"

"Take us with you! Please! Help us!"

"They're gonna fuckin' eat us! Please help us!"

George let it all out: "Fuck you! *Fuck you!*"

He shot both of the boys in both of their knees. Both cried out in agonizing pain. The zombies vocalized something in response, almost in harmony with the agonizing cries, the vibrations of their screams resonating in the bodies of the walking dead.

George leaned against the Cavalier and put his hands on his face. He began to cry over the screams of the dying and the moans of the dead. His soul was sad, knowing the new world forming around him was replacing the old George with some kind of animal, a beast who was out of his mind.

Pulling himself together after a moment's release, George reloaded his gun.

The creatures were seconds away as George sat down in the driver's seat and caught his breath.

He started the car. He looked to his left. Clear, apart from the two frat boys who were making a futile and painful effort to move away from the advancing horde.

He looked straight ahead. Clear.

He looked to his right. No bat this time. All clear.

George closed the door and shifted to first as several

of the zombies began to wail. More figures were walking from the plaza toward the bodies even as the first wave had already arrived. George heard the final screams of the frat boys as the zombies began to eat their flesh.

George drove away while the zombies devoured the Betas.

# Chapter 9

The sunny morning sky held up an array of puffy, healthy white clouds. Birds glided in the wind. Butterflies flew across the highway as George drove along. He was surprised to see so many ghouls along the road. For every mile, there seemed to be at least three zombies stumbling along.

George was halfway between San Marcos and New Braunfels when something caught his eye. In stark contrast to the barren road and serene countryside, George spotted what he thought was some sort of military checkpoint. As he began to slow to a stop, camouflaged and heavily armed soldiers walking around the barrier confirmed it was indeed a checkpoint.

George was now face to face with Homeland Security.

A large red gate with concertina wire stood next to a small tower. Sandbags were stacked on both sides of the tower and gate. Two large concrete slabs, very much like the kind utilized to divide freeways, were in front of the sandbags. A soldier was in a booth below the tower and several other soldiers stood behind the barrier. Behind the point, two Humvees with cattle trailers were parked.

The guard in the tower alerted the others to the Cavalier's presence. Several soldiers readied their weapons. The guard in the tower called over a megaphone to George.

"Halt. To the driver of the black vehicle. Halt. Do not move or attempt to leave."

Five soldiers advanced through the now open gate, machine guns trained on the vehicle.

A butterfly landed on the Cavalier's windshield wiper.

"You are not under attack. We are operatives of FEMA and Homeland Security. We are here to help."

George was cursing under his breath. He could put it in reverse and head another way, risking the soldiers firing on his vehicle and, more than likely, finishing him off.

A shot rang out. George flinched. A zombie near the car fell flat on its face.

The soldiers edged closer.

"Exit your vehicle with your hands behind your head. Lay face down on the ground."

*Goddammit*, thought George. He considered the notion of jumping out of his car and running away on foot, but he knew it was a dumb choice. There was an obvious bullet-ridden conclusion if he went with *that* decision.

The soldiers surrounded the vehicle.

The butterfly flew away.

"Non-compliance will result in neutralization."

A soldier opened the driver's-side door.

The bottom line was, in George's mind, that he wasn't going to get any closer to home as a puddle of blood, so he chose to cooperate.

Forcing George's hands behind his head, the soldiers dragged him out of the car and placed him face down on the ground. A soldier then brought George's hands down to the back of his waist and cuffed him with a heavy duty zip tie.

For his protection, of course.

Dust jumped into George's eyes as he hit the ground. He tried to blink it away, but couldn't.

He was then frisked and relieved of his wallet and his money.

One of the soldiers picked him up and led him away while the other four searched his vehicle. One acted as guard, capping the occasional zombie that shambled along, protecting the other three during their search of the Cavalier.

George was placed in the back of one of the cattle trailers behind the Hummers. He was given a bottle of water and very sarcastically told the giver, "Gee, that's so generous of you."

George sat in the trailer for over an hour before three new soldiers approached. One opened the back of the trailer, the other two trained their rifles on George. He didn't like it so much and commented, "Is that really necessary? The whole gun pointing thing?"

The unarmed soldier smugly replied, "It's for your protection and mine, sir."

"Sure it is," responded George.

"My name is Corporal Robert Johnson. I am a member of Homeland Security. I'm here to ask you some questions."

Johnson was wearing the usual digital gray camouflage fatigues, with lots of various gear strapped around his waist and over his shoulders. He had a moustache and a buzz cut. He had pulled out a pen and a small blue notepad.

"Now, sir, your driver's license shows that you are from Austin. Why have you not joined the FEMA centers up there as you have been ordered over the radio?"

"Don't trust ya'll, sir," replied George swiftly.

After a bewildered look, Johnson made a note in the notepad. "What are you doing so far away from Austin?"

"Want to get home, sir."

"Where's home?"

"San Uvalde."

"Never heard of it."

"Seventy miles west of San Antonio."

"Doesn't matter, no one is allowed on the roads anymore. FEMA and the U.S. Military have full control. The U.S. has been put in a state of emergency."

"Always has been since the 'War Powers Act' anyway. So what else is new?"

"Excuse me?" replied Johnson, puzzled at the remark.

"Never mind," said George.

Johnson made another notation in his book. "Tell me where you got your weapons from."

"Pistol's mine. Machine gun was given to me in San Marcos."

"Why do you have them?"

George made a face, but then answered, "Protection, sir.

Seems the world is a little more dangerous today than it was a couple of days ago, don't you think?"

Johnson jotted down a few more notes. A shot rang out. The four looked away for a moment, listened, then looked back at their business.

Johnson stood up. "Thank you, sir, we appreciate your cooperation."

"Am I free to go sir?" asked George.

"No sir, you will be joining the locals at the New Braunfels FEMA center this evening at seven before it—"

"—Gets dark. Yeah, I know," interrupted George. "What about my car?"

"It's going to be impounded. You can retrieve it from FEMA after the state of emergency is over and you are released from the camp."

"Fine, fine," said George. "Can I at least have my wife's photo back? It's in my wallet. You know, where my money *used to be?*"

Johnson reached into his pocket, retrieved the wallet, searched through it until he found the photo, then removed the photo and tucked it into George's breast pocket. He then said, "There you go, sir."

Sneering contemptuously at George, the three soldiers closed the back of the trailer and locked it. Johnson told them, "Mark him as a red square when you get to the camp. Firearms possession, possible looter, possible insurgent."

They walked away.

George was locked in the cattle trailer for the rest of the day while soldiers manned the checkpoint. He was given two bottles of water and a protein bar in the early afternoon. When he needed to piss, he was followed by a soldier. Always at gunpoint.

Just before it got dark, two soldiers manned the Hummer that the trailer was tied to. Alone in the back, George began the trip to the FEMA camp.

As night threw its black pall over Texas, George and the vehicle approached the FEMA camp in New Braunfels. The camouflaged Hummer was crossing the land at quite a clip. Along the way, the trooper manning the mounted gun was blasting zombies every now and then. Some of the shells tapped across the aluminum top of the trailer as George sat in the back. It wasn't the most comfortable ride he ever took, and he wondered how the horses and other cattle that once rode in the back might have felt. He was surprised that FEMA had had the courtesy to clean out the requisitioned trailer, but the aroma of barnyard excrement still floated around George's nose.

A bright light began to shine through the gaps in the trailer. George stood up to look through the gaps. He figured he was on the loop that circled the outskirts of New Braunfels because the lights of one of the high school stadiums seemed to be the direction they were headed.

FEMA had set up shop at the stadium. Hordes of zombies had massed around the stadium, spread out and unconcentrated, but in numbers.

Watching.

Clawing.

Waiting.

George remembered this stadium. It was the home of his

personal archenemies, the New Braunfels Titans. George remembered in his youth when the Titans defeated the San Uvalde Marauders in the regional football playoffs. George was only in fourth grade, but he knew his cousin Aaron was on the team. Aaron was one of the stars of the team, playing wingback. He had sprinter speed and was skillful when handed the ball. George even kept the spirit ribbon his mother bought for him many years ago as a bitter memento of the sound defeat at the hands of the Titans.

George had his chance to take on his personal enemy on the gridiron when he was a senior in high school. Getting a chance to get a piece of the team that beat his cousin years ago was like a dream come true. George even went so far as to memorize from the scouting reports the names of the players he would be lined up against. During the game, George called out their names, promising a beheading.

The game was close, but the San Uvalde secondary was exploited by the quarterback, who kept the game in the air. The San Uvalde team was holding them on the ground, and even initiated their own ground attack. When it was over, San Uvalde had handed New Braunfels their first scoring touchdown on the ground for their season, though it wasn't enough. San Uvalde lost 21–14.

But George got a chance to bash his personal enemies. It was a moment he would never forget.

The vehicle came to a stop by a gate near the stadium and began to open fire on the zombies near the gate. George watched them fall like slabs of meat to the ground. Once the area was clear, the gate was somehow mechanically opened, and the Hummer entered through the sandbagged and concertina-wired chain link fence, crushing the bodies of the dead. George was thrown around in the back of the trailer, banging up against the side. He knew they must be in as the jostling by the undead/dead speed bumps stopped. He sat up and watched through the gaps as the gate closed, moments before any zombie could get in. The Humvee drove down a secured alleyway and came to another gate. It was opened after someone monitored the security. The gunner would have taken care of any monster that had beat the gate.

The camp, so it seemed, was secure again.

It was quite a lot for George to take in as he was led out of the back of the trailer. Along the fence line that spread all the way around the stadium were several towers, manned and armed. Spotlights shined into the darkness outside the stadium like holy weapons cutting through the dark evil of the accursed night. Sandbags lined the gates, close to six feet high. The sizzle sound coming from the gates indicated to George that the fence was electrified.

George was led to the ticket booth that was the entrance to another gated area, one that ran the perimeter of the track around the football field, but immediately in front of the bleachers. The fence was high and concertina-wired. There were sandbags on the outside, but not on the inside, where thousands of locals had been unwillingly gathered. It was a fenced-off area within a fenced-off area. Civilians in the center, soldiers in the middle. Zombies, obviously, outside.

Standing by a ticket booth near yet another door with a small tower looming above, George, still cuffed, was digitally photographed. Moments later, he was given an ID tag. His face, his name and his social security number were on it, along with a big read square. He was told that he was to wear it at all times. Not wearing the tag would result in neutralization.

The guard clipped the tag to the pocket of George's flannel.

George was then led through the chain-linked door into a small fenced-off area about the size of the average bathroom. The door in front of him seemed to be locked magnetically. The door behind him was shut and locked. A guard on the other side of that door trained a machine gun on him as did a soldier in the tower right by the ticket booth and containment area. Looking ahead, George got his first glimpse of the people of the camp. There were many gathered by the magnetic door. Various voices were saying, "Fresh meat," "We got a wetback here," and "Another one for the Fours." It was hard for George to concentrate on anything as there was so much to pay attention to.

"Step to the white X, please," commanded a voice from the tower. Looking to the ground, George found the X. He stepped on it. "Face away from the gate please." George obeyed, and a hand came through a small opening in the gate and cut the zip tie that had been bruising his wrists. George rubbed his wrists, still red from the bonds. A voice from behind told him to turn again. He was handed a blanket and a pillow.

The voice from the tower boomed, "Citizens by the gate, you have ten seconds to back away from the magnetic gate. Noncompliance will result in neutralization."

Quickly the people moved, though several made some uncomplimentary remarks under their breath. Most walked away from the gate entirely, while several stayed in the vicinity.

After confirmation of security, the magnetic gate buzzed open and George entered the camp. The gate then promptly closed behind him. Another buzz locked the door once again.

Gazing into the mass of people that littered the interior of the stadium, George couldn't believe his eyes. There were so many people around him. It reminded him of being at a rock concert, but he figured no band would be playing today.

Several people were glaring at him as he passed by them and into the throbbing mass of people in the center. The field, from what he could see, seemed to be split into sections. At each end zone and around the track there were several large tents set up. The field itself seemed wide open, with no tents but plenty of people. George noticed again how secure the bleachers were from the people on the field: electrified and razor wired. It seemed to effectively separate the people from the military. Soldiers populated the bleachers and the press boxes on both sides. Though it was assumed they should be guarding the place and the civilians, most seemed to be drinking or napping.

"New here?"

The question took George by surprise. He turned to see a large white guy standing behind him. He was wearing a black shirt, cowboy boots, and blue jeans. The shirt had a Confederate flag on the front, faded, but still worn proudly.

The man continued, "You need to head over to the other end zone, 'cause Mexicans aren't allowed on this end."

Taken aback by the remark, George responded, "Well, good thing I was born a Texan. But if I see a Mexican, I'll be sure to tell them to tell you to go fuck yourself."

The man started to stomp toward George when a girl came between them. "Josh, stop it," she said to the big man. "Leave him alone. You're going to get in trouble and they'll red square you!"

Josh glared at the girl, then looked at George. "You watch your ass."

"Aw, fuck off," said George as he turned around and walked away.

After an hour or two of wandering around the place (and losing his blanket and pillow in the process), George figured he found the area where food was served. It was along the track on the visitor side under a large blue tent. He also figured out where the medics would be, on the home track under a red tent. Most of the other tents were for the military and internal guards. He noticed several packs of soldiers patrolling the area, machine guns at ready.

George was a bit discouraged, standing near the thirty-yard line on the home side. Finding a place to sit or lie down wasn't easy, as many people in the facility had already claimed a spot in what seemed to be a sleeping area near the forty-yard line on the visitors side of the field. Instead, George looked around at all the faces. Many young and many old. Many seemed sick or hungry. Even in the cool spring night, the wind couldn't blow away the body odor.

Behind each of the end zones near the gates were ten portable restrooms. Deciding he would need to explore more to find a place to rest, George started walking again.

Just as he began his stroll, a voice called to him.

"Hey, you. In the flannel."

George turned and saw the girl who had kept Josh at bay almost two hours earlier. She had short bleached blond hair, very thin, but a complement to her elfish face. A small curved nose sat below two bright blue eyes and above her thin lips. She was slender and her body was soft. She was wearing a light blue overall outfit that was cut short. A white shirt was underneath. White shoes and lacy ankle socks rounded out her attire. She was very cute, though seemed very young despite being just outside twenty years of age.

After a moment of taking her in, George quickly responded, "Look, I don't want any trouble."

"No trouble. Just thought I'd apologize for my brother. He's kind of a prick."

Wanting to comment on that remark, George instead said, "I accept your apology. I forgive your brother."

She extended her hand to George. "I'm Misty."

George accepted her soft hand. "George. Charmed." He gave a small, chivalrous nod in lieu of a bow, then motioned around and asked, "So what's the story here, Misty?"

"It sucks, that's the story," she replied.

George chuckled politely. They began to stroll around and among the people in the stadium.

Misty explained, "At first the soldiers and medical people

were real nice. People started coming in around three days ago. A lot were gathered by the military that afternoon."

George passed two kids. One was playing a handheld video game. The other was watching.

"Anyway," continued Misty, "They were very helpful and nice to everybody. But yesterday, the medical people just up and left. There's some sick people in here, too. A couple of people had been bit and were very sick."

"You mean they're still in here?"

"Yeah. They're with their families."

"Misty, don't they know that they're dead already? The bite gives them the infection."

"I know, but the family won't let anyone near."

"Fuckin' stupid if you ask me."

They strolled in silence for a second, watching the people bustling around them. "So what else?"

"Well, along with the medics, soldiers started leaving too. There's not as many now as there were before. We don't feel so safe now. Especially . . ." Misty paused.

"Especially what?" asked George.

They passed a young girl who was in the embrace of her mother, both wrapped in a blanket, both weeping.

"Especially when they started taking girls. Little ones, teenagers, ones that wouldn't put up a fight. Ones without families to stick up for them."

"What are you talking about?" asked George, though he knew the probable answer.

"They'd take them to the locker rooms over behind the fence. Over there by the port-a-potties."

"Aw, fuckin' shit, man," said George, "That's bullshit. How can the people stand for that? The way it seems, we could take them if we wanted to." He gestured at all the people.

"They've got so many guns, we couldn't do anything without getting shot. And anyway, everyone still feels safe. Except for the . . . ," Misty stopped again. She looked at George's ID tag.

"Dammit, Misty, just tell me, all right!"

"Except for the red squares. A couple of times a day, the inner guards round up a few, take them up the bleachers, and toss them outside the gate from the top of the press box. My uncle Brandon says they're saving ammunition."

George looked at his tag and gulped. After a moment, he changed the subject. "The way it looks to me, though, is that everyone is either sick or hungry." They passed an elderly couple. The old man was helping the old woman drink from a tin water cup. Misty nodded her head in agreement. George asked, "What about food? Do they still feed ya'll?"

"They put food out under those tents," Misty replied, pointing. "But stronger people get in first, bullying people in line, leaving little to nothing for us. The weak want to leave, but can't. The strong want to stay for as long as possible."

"Won't be long at this rate," George mumbled.

"What's worse is the people in here have started forming gangs. From day one. They've claimed sections of the field. The big ones are in each of the four corners of the field."

"What do they do?"

"They've been beating up people, taking their food and money. It sucks."

"Your brother?"

"He's a Three."

"Three?"

Misty pointed in the general direction of the corners. "One, two, three, four."

"Oh, okay," said George.

"The Ones are mainly regular people who don't want any trouble. Most of the people officially or unofficially belong to them. The Twos are blacks, Threes whites, Fours 'meskins.'"

George winced at the dialect.

"The middle of the field is supposed to be neutral ground. But mostly they all just pick fights with each other."

"And if you don't want in?"

"Then you get fucked up anyway," boomed a voice from behind them. It was Josh. "You need to keep your wetback ass away from my sister and head over to the Fours if you know what's good for you."

An Asian guy walked by George. George grabbed him by the arm.

"Hey man, what's your name?"

The man was a bit rattled, but responded, "Eric."

George then looked at Josh. "What about Eric? Where does he go?"

Josh was dumbfounded for a moment. "Uhh . . ."

Misty chuckled.

Josh backhanded her. "It's not funny, Misty!" he yelled.

George delivered a solid shot to Josh's crotch, burying his knuckles deep and doubling the big galoot over. As an afterthought, George clutched Josh's head and drove two fierce knees against his skull. The second one sent Josh to the ground.

"Josh!" screamed Misty. She turned to George. "You need to go. The Threes will be looking for you."

A crowd began to gather. Before George could run, Misty grabbed his arm. She whispered, "Thank you," then let him go into the crowd.

Finding a black-and-white blanket on the ground, George threw it over his red flannel like a cape and looked for a spot to hide somewhere in the crowd.

Hide and lie down.

Lie down and sleep.

Sleep and dream.

Esparanza was standing in front of George on a highway. She was wearing what looked like a blue shirt and white shorts. She was barefoot. Cars were wrecked all along the road. A vehicle sped by George. Esparanza began to giggle. George felt happy. Teasing, she raised her right hand and made a gesture with her index finger for George to come closer. George tried to move closer, but couldn't. He was stuck. She began to run. George began to run, but fell. He got up, but fell again. When he looked up, Esparanza was looming over him like a giant. She ran toward a burning city in the distance and stomped it with her bare foot. Her foot began to bleed. She stomped the city again. Blood began to cover the ground near George's feet. She pointed down into the city and said, "There!"

George was jarred from his sleep by a gentle, but firm, kick to the ribs. He looked up. Three Hispanic guys hovered over him under the cool morning sky. Two had to be teens.

One was a man. The two kids were wearing plaid shirts open at the collar, revealing their white tank top shirts underneath. The big guy had a goatee, a hair net, and a black tank top–style shirt. All three wore loose khakis and black shoes.

"Morning guys," said George.

"Is that him?" asked the man.

"That's him, Marco," replied the kid in the green plaid shirt.

"*Ey*," said Marco, "Jose said that you punked one of the Threes, *esse*."

"I don't know what you're talking about," said George, rubbing his eyes and sitting up. The blanket rolled off him, revealing his flannel he forgot he was hiding.

"That's him. He was wearing that. I remember," said Jose, pointing at the flannel.

A crowd was gathering around.

"You saw someone else, dude," George urgently replied.

"It was you, *esse*," said Jose. "He's a red square, too, Marco."

"Why you lying, *buey*," asked Marco in a distinct south Texas dialect. The crowd grew larger.

George got to his feet and stretched the stretch of a man who just woke up—the stretch of a man hiding his fear. Maybe not fear for the two punks, but for Marco. He looked intimidating.

"Man, look," said George, "I don't want any trouble and I don't want to fuckin' join any of the corners."

"You know you're a red square, right? You know what that means, right?" asked Marco.

Having a pretty good idea what it meant, George

responded, "Look, I don't give a shit what color my fuckin' square is, just leave me the fuck alone!" The tension was building in George quickly. The patience of the old George was replaced by belligerence. Having fought for his life several times already, watched people die and taken some lives for survival's sake, he was becoming edgier, quicker to fight, to challenge. Confident. The chip was clearly on his shoulder, and he was daring someone to knock it off. The animal within him was waiting to pounce.

Frustrated, Marco replied, "I'm tired of this *culo's* attitude. Jose, Pedro, kick his ass."

The two kids spread out, fists raised, and circled George. The crowd began to cheer and yell.

Soldiers in the stands took notice. They readied their weapons.

So did the Corners. Several members from each group except the Ones were sent out to investigate.

George sighed, not wanting to fight, but feeling its inevitability.

*Is this what the world has come to?* he thought. *Fighting among people in a world falling apart exponentially just yards away from them?* It was all right, though. George had enough bitter rage to go around.

He scoped things out, focused on Pedro, and as both lunged in, George committed to a flying knee, cracking Pedro in the jaw. Pedro fell and Jose hesitated a step, watching his buddy fall face first on the grassy football field. As George landed on his feet, he quickly delivered a right back fist toward Jose. The hesitation saved Jose from catching it on his cheek, but now he stood in front of the man that just

KO'd his friend. A twinge of fear teased Jose's heart as he started throwing a flurry of punches at George. After taking three shots to the face, George ducked under the flying fists and shot for Jose's waist, securing a side waistlock. Jose sent an informal elbow attack toward George's face, connecting above his eye. But it was not enough to stop the arching throw George had begun, sending Jose backward, tossing him awkwardly on his head and neck. Jose's own weight and the force of the throw damaged his neck and the resulting pain immobilized the young thug. George was going to continue the assault, but after seeing Jose grab at his own neck and cry out in pain, he knew it was done. The crowd went crazy.

George stood up, blood flowing over his right eye. "You go tell whoever the fuck you need to tell that I ain't standing for this shit!" George yelled in the full glory of his anger and frustration. "Stay the fuck away! Do you hear me?!" Marco stood in stunned silence. "You fuckin' hear me, Marco?!"

Marco nodded. Someone from the crowd took a pot shot at Marco, slapping him across the back of his head. Before he knew it, Marco was getting jumped by what seemed to be a group of Twos. Others began to kick the boys on the ground—mostly Twos, but a little bit of everyone got a shot in.

*Goddamit!* George thought. *What the fuck is wrong with these people?!*

A small group of Fours had arrived, as well as a group of Threes, simultaneously. They took in the sights, both realizing they were there for George. More Twos jumped them both before they could get to George. The energy and motion around the area now was intense as people were scrambling for position.

George was appalled. *I can't believe this,* he thought. *I'm about to die in a gang fight in a FEMA camp in New Braunfels fuckin' Texas.* He shook his head, trembling with fear and sadness. His breathing became erratic.

"George!" yelled Misty, who had appeared suddenly. "Hurry! This way!" Her soft hand grabbed George's and pulled him out of the pandemonium that was erupting.

As she led him swiftly away, a full blown riot erupted on the field. Fists, objects, and bludgeons were flying. Those not involved moved in a wave away from the brawl in the direction of the closest end zone. A large mass of people remained in the middle, fists flying.

Within seconds, several members of the military personnel in the bleachers who had been watching the events unfold opened fire on the brawlers. Bullets diced hands, cut arms, pierced legs, stabbed brains, and chopped faces indiscriminately. However, another group of soldiers began to fire on the soldiers who were neutralizing the fighters, disagreeing extremely with their comrades' actions. It was clear there was no leadership among the governmental protectors. The surviving brawlers began to scatter, as did the soldiers, who were now engaged in a firefight in the stands with each other.

Outside the gates, the commotion was attracting the attention of scores of zombies. It was as if they could smell the blood, wishing for the red mists spit out of the breathing bodies by bullets to fall on their tongues like a satanic snowfall dropping on the mouths of the children of the

Inferno. The frenzy of death was resonating through their dead heads like a ranch hand ringing an iron triangle for supper.

They were watching.

Waiting.

It was an awkward afternoon. A large pile of bodies lay in the middle of Titan field, and the bodies of over a dozen soldiers lay in the aluminum bleachers of both the visitors' side and the home side of the field. For several hours after the morning skirmish, things were quiet. But desperation was beginning to rear its ugly head around the facility.

With the gang numbers drastically reduced, a truce was called by the Ones and agreed to by all but the Threes. Then, two hours after the massacre, the Ones, Twos, and Fours united and wiped out what was left of the Threes.

The soldiers didn't respond.

Breakfast was not served this particular morning. Many were left wondering if lunch would be.

Finding an unoccupied medical tent, Misty and George sat and hid. George was probably safe due to the gang truce, but probably not from the guards. That is, the guards that were left. If they decided to search for him, having a place to hide would be a good idea. The medical tent was a good enough place as any, even if it was close to the bleachers.

Misty had left George alone for a few minutes and returned with some cloth and healing ointments so she could tend to the cut over his eye. She helped him remove his flannel. Sitting in front of each other, she tended to the wound above his eye. His adrenaline was gone, so the pain was very perceptible. He winced, but gritted his teeth and allowed her gentle hands to continue working.

Her blue eyes sparkled. "You were very brave out there," she said.

George responded, "I don't know about brave so much as I was scared. I was so scared. Pissed off, too."

"Why?"

"Just, these people, you know? They can't get along, even when they need to the most. One group thinks they know what's best for the other and insists on babying them—and what a shitty job they've done up to now, huh? The others can't even unite against them. They'd rather divide themselves and fight and kill each other. It's such bullshit," George said, gritting his teeth again as Misty placed a patch soaked with medicine on George's cut.

"Hush now," she whispered. "It's all right."

Her voice began to calm him, though he remained a bit grouchy. "Man, I wish it was. I wish we could unite against that shit outside . . . Those dead things."

As Misty secured the patch over the cut, she bowed her head. "I'm so sorry, George."

George sulked. "It's not your fault."

Misty finished with the primitive bandage. She kissed it. "There, now you're all better." She looked into George's eyes. Her blue eyes were hard to resist. She touched his face. George's hands moved across her thighs. Both began to breathe in a different way; energy began to manifest.

George gazed into her eyes and felt an almost magnetic pull toward her. He wanted to kiss her. He wanted to grope her and rub his hands all over her body. He could feel her desire.

But he was scared. Not of kissing her or anything in regards to his physical attraction to her, but of the reality of the situation. Sure, he had shared himself with Keri with reckless passion, but so much had happened since then. The fear that humanity wasn't going to survive this plague. That they could not unite and help each other. That if humanity united, another segment of that same humanity would rise up and crush them, like they did to Jeff and the barrier people.

George wondered, *Hasn't it always been that way? Divided? Segregated? United, but really not? Even the Civil War was one group of people who had the right to separate, but were made to stay together by force.*

George knew it would be hard to get home, but never thought it would be *this* hard. After today, it seemed hopeless. No vehicle. No weapons. No food. No water.

George leaned in to Misty and held her. She embraced him as he began to weep. He wanted to see his mom and family again, but was now afraid they were dead, and all this danger he had encountered was for naught. He began to shake, a latent shock surfacing.

Pulling himself together, George shared a kiss on the cheek with Misty. A moist sensation touched his lips as he kissed away a tear from her cheek. She returned the affection with a short, sweet kiss on his lips. She wiped his tears away. He wiped hers. Perhaps she was feeling the same way.

As they separated, a man pulled open the curtain to

the tent. George and Misty's hearts skipped a beat. Misty gasped.

"Uncle Brandon!" she exclaimed, jumping to her feet and embracing the man. He was tall and rather big and sported a green John Deere hat. Suspenders held up a pair of worn and dirty blue jeans that were fighting a waist war with Uncle Brandon's prominent beer gut. The gut was stretching his extra-extra large Charlie Daniels shirt to the limit. Misty, in all her dainty charm, jumped and hugged him around his thick neck, cheek to cheek.

They both smiled.

Though his gut suggested bad physical conditioning, he seemed to have the strength—if not the power—of a man of size.

"How you been, sweetie-pie?" he asked, kissing her on the cheek.

"I've been all right, Uncle Brandon." She turned to George. "This is my friend, George."

George stood and offered his hand. "Nice to meet you, sir."

"Likewise, good sir," replied Brandon, showing a smile. "I hear you whipped some of them spics' asses this morning. We could use someone like you."

"What do you mean?" George asked. "If it's about joining a gang, forget it!"

"No, no, it's nothing like that," he said, pulling out a pack of Red Man and stuffing some chaw in his bottom lip. "Well, me and my son, Brandon Junior, are planning on making a break for it."

"Are you crazy?" asked Misty. "They'll kill you!"

"Hang on, Misty," said George. "Hear him out."

They all took a seat. Misty surprised George by sitting on his lap. They glanced at each other quickly. George became a bit excited. Uncle Brandon winced, but shook his head and shared his idea.

"First off, their numbers are low now. A lot of them have been taking off, leaving their posts. Way I see it, they're not unified anymore. And it definitely seems like they have no leadership anymore. Secondly, they're looking for you, George. I heard they're going to do another roundup. Why, in God's name, I don't know. But I'm going to report you."

"What?!" George gasped, taken aback.

Misty exclaimed, "Uncle Brandon!"

Brandon lifted a hand to show he wasn't finished explaining, then continued, "I'm going to report you because when those two guys get over here, we're going to jump 'em and take their guns!"

"Sounds crazy," George said. The plan was simple—perhaps too simple—but could he really expect for some brilliant strategy to come along? He figured he'd rather do something desperate than do nothing at all, though it was still a big risk. He asked, "What do you have in mind?"

"We lead them here to this tent and jump them."

"With *what?*" Misty asked.

"Well, with a brick or some shit. A pipe. *Something.*"

*Because there are a lot of bricks lying aroud,* thought George to himself.

"All right, so we find something to bash them with, pound them, then what?"

"We take their guns, make like we're not carrying

anything, and head to the ticket booth. Someone could act the fool and get them to open that magnetic door. Then, we take out the tower guy first, secure the open door, and take out anyone else in the area."

"Then what?" asked Misty.

"It's simple. Either we find one of those Hummers with a key in it, or we make a run to our house."

"Neither of those options sound likely to happen," George pointed out. "First, we'd have to find a Hummer with the keys in it."

"Well, yeah," replied Brandon. "That's what I said."

"And, yeah, anyway," George went on, "With the run to the house—*wherever that is*—the tower guys would pick us off in a matter of seconds. That is, if the zombies didn't get us first."

"Listen, don't be such a killjoy, George," said Brandon. "What other choice do we have?"

George thought for a moment. Brandon's plan was full of holes, but George knew that any plan that would get him to San Uvalde was going to be a big risk. And, as he had already decided, he would rather do something desperate than do nothing at all.

"Well, where's Brandon Junior?" asked George.

Uncle Brandon turned toward the entrance and called out, "Brandon Junior!"

A small boy barely four feet tall entered the room. He was wearing blue jeans and a black pro-wrestling shirt, and when he spoke it was obvious that his voice was nowhere near reaching puberty. He said, "Yeah, Pa? Oh, hey, cousin Misty!"

"Hi, B.J.," Misty replied.

George was surprised at the age and size of Brandon Junior. He had expected someone a lot older.

"You ready for this, son?" Brandon asked.

"Yeah, Pa. I'm ready," replied the short kid, though his red mullet and freckles hardly hid his fear.

"All right, Junior, this is what we're going to do—"

Yet before they could even begin phase one of their plan, several screams broke the conspirators' concentration. Every head turned to the tent opening. George looked at Misty, confused. Everyone rushed outside the tent.

When they emerged into the open air, they witnessed a mass of people running away from the east end of the stadium near the land of the Ones and Twos.

Uncle Brandon grabbed one of the people who were running. "Hey, you! What the hell's going on?!"

The person, a blond man with thinning hair, shivering and scared, cried, "It's the Garrisons! The ones that were dying from bites infected the rest of their family and a bunch of others! Now they're all coming after us! Let go of me!" The man broke loose from Brandon with a yank of his arm and ran off toward the ticket booth.

George looked toward the end zone where all the action was happening. Sure enough, several creatures were attacking some of the incarcerated civilians and the civilians were fighting back with little to no success. Several people were already being feasted upon, while others were being quickly snatched by undead hands. Teeth sunk into flesh as the zombies feasted and the victims began their transformation.

Gunfire erupted near the ticket booth area as some of the

soldiers tried to stop the advance of the people. But everyone knew that with creatures inside the perimeter, the safest place was in the area with the soldiers.

George looked to see two interior soldiers slowly walking toward the slaughter, guns trained on the creatures. Already, several of the devoured dead were rising. Close to twenty zombies, including the Garrisons, were marching toward the fleeing crowd. Several ghouls remained, devouring the inhabitants who tried to fend the creatures off.

It seemed that the brevity of the attempts to impede the zombies from infecting the captives and the non-responsiveness of the guards led to the mayhem. It didn't take long for the chaos to erupt.

The end of the FEMA camp was close at hand. If George and his newfound friends were going to make a break for it, now was the perfect chance.

"Brandon, this is it," George said. "We have to make our move."

They all knew he was right. They tensed up as adrenaline coursed through their veins.

George knelt down and yanked a tent spike from the ground, brushed the dirt from the end, and made certain he had a firm grip.

Misty yanked a board away from a picnic table. It appeared long enough to do damage, yet short enough not to be cumbersome.

Brandon found a lead pipe, one of the supports of the tent. It was bent in some places, but was good enough on short notice.

Brandon Junior chipped off a loose and large chunk of cement from the exterior lining of the track.

The four of them, shuffling through the panicked and clearing crowd, crept toward the soldiers, who had now begun opening controlled fire on the zombies.

George and Misty overwhelmed one of the guards while the two Brandons did the same to the other. Uncle Brandon tackled his guard to the ground, but B.J. hesitated to join the fray. "C'mon, Junior," said Uncle Brandon, "Hit 'em. Hit 'em, now." B.J. shook in fear, his eyes bulging before engaging in smashing the soldier's skull to mush.

George planted the spike deep in the sternum of the second soldier. George and Uncle Brandon then went about securing the soldiers' weapons and digging through their pockets for extra ammo.

Misty moved to B.J. "You going to be all right?"

There was no verbal answer, but when B.J. grabbed her and held her in a warm and quivering embrace, she knew the answer. His hands, now deflowered of their innocence, left streaks of blood stains on her back.

"Misty," said Uncle Brandon. "Take these canteens."

Sadly, Misty peeled B.J. from her embrace. "Wait here, B.J." she said as she moved to take the canteens of water.

The creatures began to shuffle toward the retreating crowd, getting closer and closer to George's group.

A gunshot from the visitors' bleachers tore open a hole in Brandon Junior's chest, exiting out the back. Another tore open his right leg. Another to the arm.

Quickly, Uncle Brandon aimed his requisitioned rifle

toward the visitors' bleachers and cut down the only two soldiers that were paying attention to the interior soldiers and the zombies on the field. George quickly followed his example, taking out three soldiers on the home bleachers, one of which was firing back. The three soldiers then fell, seirously wounded and unable to fire their weapons.

Uncle Brandon moved to his fallen son. "B.J., you okay?"

B.J. cringed in pain, weeping the final tears of the dying. He was about to leave the mortal world with an infinite fear, a sad confusion melded with a pain he would never feel again.

Uncle Brandon heaved Brandon Junior over his shoulder with one arm and yelled, "The ticket booth! It's our only chance!"

As Misty and Uncle Brandon began to run to the crowded ticket booth exit, George got to a knee and took out the guards in the nearest towers with a shot to the head. The soldiers who had been manning the other towers around the facility had already abandoned their posts. Safe from the gun towers, George ran to rejoin his group.

The zombies, growing in number, began to advance on the crowd. Though they were nearly eighty yards away on the other side of the field, their presence was a new threat. It meant there was now a battle on two fronts.

After firing and cutting down several civilians, the remaining soldiers gave up and retreated in the direction of the Hummers. The gates began to pop and sizzle as several civilians threw blankets on the electrified fence in an attempt to create a crude insulator. After several group efforts they were able to collapse the gate, causing it to crumple to the ground.

Those wearing shoes stepped across it. The barefooted took their chances. Several people fell on exposed areas of the gate and roasted on the metal.

The zombies on the field were getting closer as one of the Hummers started to drive off. Three or four people jumped on the vehicle. One soldier tried to man the gun, but was overpowered by two men and thrown overboard. Several camp members took boots to the man, beating him into unconsciousness.

The Hummer sped to the vehicle entrance, smashing through the first locked gate with ease. A mass of people followed the machine through the crushed entrance. Two people were still on the hood; two were at the guns. One opened fire on the zombies around the fence as the other tried to work his way to the driver seat. The vehicle barreled to the second gate which led directly to the parking lot. The Humvee busted through the gate, knocking the zombies in front out of the way like bowling pins and crushing them under the chainlinked gate and the wheels of the war machine. The people of the facility ran right behind it, taking a shot at freedom, prepared to risk the army of zombies outside.

With the two men on the hood, the driver could not see the vehicle that was still in the parking lot of the stadium. It rear-ended the '98 Honda Accord, sending the two guys on the hood flying. One smashed into the back window of the Accord, jarring his neck, glass tearing into his back. The other flew over the vehicle and smashed his head on the pavement near the handicapped parking sign.

Both were promptly devoured.

The driver's head smashed against the window, creating a

weblike circle in the glass. The man trying to get in was also sent flying into a group of creatures. They tore into his flesh, his screams buried by the cries of the liberated, yet endangered, facility members.

The man in the gunner position started opening fire on everything that moved, both facility people and zombies, before being engulfed by the undead when his ammo ran out. The creatures made a buffet of all the flesh brought down by friendly fire.

It was a veritable free-for-all as the last mass of people forced their way through the gate, pushing aside as many creatures as they could. The exit was severely congested with people and zombies as the second Hummer, facility people hanging all over it, tried to force its way over the mass of humanity bottlenecked at the gate. The entrance was filled with the dead, the dying, and those still fighting for survival. The Hummer crushed a large mass of people, with cries of the alive and the dying overshadowing the howls of the already dead and reanimated.

The vehicle got stuck as it tried to work its way over the bodies. The tires dug in and ground several bodies of the dying and undead into the asphalt. Blood and bone shot from the tires, spraying the people still trying to escape with a red mist that peppered their faces like a paintbrush flicking paint from its bristles. Several alive and dying began to roast on the fence near the vehicular and human collision, their flesh turning a dark red, their clothes igniting. Fire danced across the burning bodies.

Misty could not believe her eyes as the remaining soldiers—the last bastion of American defense—ruthlessly pulverized both the alive and the undead with their vehicles in the driveway.

As the third Hummer began its advance to the entrance, a clean shot from George took out the gunner, who had been firing upon the last of the inmates who were trying to overtake the vehicle. Uncle Brandon immediately followed with a clean shot to the driver's head, bringing the vehicle to a sudden stop against a concrete post holding up the bleachers. Uncle Brandon then shot the soldier in the passenger seat as George dragged out the driver's body.

Uncle Brandon opened the passenger door and threw the dead soldier to the ground with one hand as he shoved Misty into the vehicle and George manned the driver seat. He was surprised to find the vehicle did not need a key, but had a switch that was moved to an on position before adjusting to start the engine.

Outside the vehicle, a creature grabbed Brandon Junior from Uncle Brandon's shoulder and dragged the corpse to the ground. Uncle Brandon turned around and decked the creature, breaking its spine, sending the monster to the ground, but not before four more quickly took its place. Uncle Brandon slammed the passenger door shut as a zombie grabbed the same arm and bit into it.

Misty screamed, "Uncle Brandon!"

Wrestling the creature to the ground and stomping on its head, Uncle Brandon yelled, "Forget me! Just go! I love you sweetie-pie!" before another creature grabbed him by the shoulders and bit into his neck. Blood splashed the side of the vehicle and ran down his neck as flesh was torn away from his body. He screamed. Misty screamed.

George backed out of the hole and shifted gears, scared and upset. Shifting to first, the Hummer moved out.

Several creatures had already begun to consume Brandon Junior's body as Uncle Brandon went down swinging. He was able to kick two creatures off his son before he was overwhelmed. He collapsed on top of his son's body, a futile yet noble attempt to protect his son's corpse from the living dead who were waiting and ready to devour them both.

Knowing the original exit would now be impossible to drive through, George blazed his own trail. Finding a weak portion of the gate, he crashed through the chain-link fence and concertina wire and then sped away through the parking lot and to the loop road.

The road by the stadium headed to 35 was relatively clear, with a majority of the creatures congregating around the stadium. Misty was sobbing uncontrollably. George drove, concentrating on the road, but shell-shocked at the horror they both barely survived. George said a quick prayer for Misty's uncle. Had it not been for Uncle Brandon closing the passenger door, Misty and George both might have been killed.

George reached for Misty's hand.

She accepted it, gripping his hand tightly, trembling.

At the stadium, zombies stalked the former military and civilian portions of the FEMA camp, searching for bodies of the recently dead. A feast of flesh was continuing in the parking lot and in the vehicle exit. Several creatures made it to the bleachers and were devouring the dead soldiers. One soldier, wounded from the rounds George fired, tried unsuccessfully to crawl away from an advancing gang. Moments later he was torn to shreds and eaten.

A small group of zombies was trying to collapse the tower by the ticket booth in order to find the source of the blood dripping from above. They were successful. The ticket booth toppled over, crushing several of their own. With spines broken and bones cracked, the creatures crushed by the tower tried to pull themselves out to no avail. Within inches of their crushed bodies, several monsters began their meal of the tower inhabitant.

Uncle Brandon and his son were torn and mutilated, their skulls cracked, their chests torn open, their innards devoured. Several zombies still sat around Uncle Brandon, tearing pieces of flesh from his large carcass. Blood dripped from their mouths. The other creatures had left Brandon Junior as a mere skeleton, hardly a speck of flesh or muscle stuck to a bone.

A majority of the inhabitants made it out of the facility alive, but half of them didn't make it across the parking lot.

One man had been trying to fight off the creatures with a pipe in the parking lot. He was overwhelmed. Two creatures bit into his face and neck. He was dragged to the ground, screaming. A creature bit into his arm. One monster grabbed his leg, which was still trying to yank itself free. Biting through the blue jeans, the monster tore at the pant leg.

A woman was being eviscerated near the bleachers. Three creatures were tearing out her innards. Blood dripped from the torn flesh, caking around the mouths of the ghouls.

Two monsters were fighting over an arm, trying to push each other to the ground.

Screams of the dying were melding with the moans of the living dead, filling the night air with woe.

The remaining half of the stadium inhabitants became infected through bites or scratches gained during the escape. Creatures had clawed at their dashing movements away from the infested stadium. Their days were numbered.

Only a lucky few made it out alive.

Alive and, for some, *alone*, but with another chance at a sunrise.

# Chapter 10

The drive to San Antonio was slower than expected, as I-35 was a mess. Cars wrecked, trucks smoldering. Bodies burned, torn, and dismembered littered the highway. Large portions of the highway proved difficult to navigate and could only be bypassed by skillful off-roading and the occasional pushing of wrecks aside by the large camouflaged Humvee. Zombies were a bit of a threat on the highway. Every once in a while, one or two would rise from a wreck and move toward the armored truck. With the slow advance through traffic, they would reach the Hummer. But since it was a military vehicle, the occasional one or two were not much of a threat after George found an opening and drove away.

Misty was still a bit of a mess, catatonic one moment, laughing the next, then weeping again. George tried to comfort her, and it did help for the most part. It had to be hard to watch close family brutally murdered like her uncle and cousin were. She seemed to be doing fine though, all things considered.

George really wasn't any better. The insanity had already shape-shifted to a bitter rage waiting to blow in his heart. He was like a string of Black Cat fireworks that would burst and pop at the light of a match.

The closer they got to San Antonio, however, the more difficult it was to travel. The cars themselves seemed lined up for oblivion, stretching deep into the city. The cars and trucks and even rigs were standing, flipped, or crashed very much like in San Marcos in front of Jeff's store.

Within the city, several fires were burning out of control in the distance. The once thriving metroplex had now become a sinister, foreboding obstacle. A dark cloud of smoke filled the skies. There even seemed to be smoke emanating from the historic "Tower of the Americas" near downtown.

As George drove under the 1604 bridge, he thought he heard something over a loudspeaker.

"Did you hear that?" he asked.

"Think so," Misty replied.

George stopped the vehicle for a moment and listened.

Looking up by the access road at the top of an embankment by an old car dealership, two camouflaged soldiers were walking down from what looked like a similar checkpoint that George was caught at in New Braunfels.

He whispered, "*Shit.*"

The voice was clearer now and was emanating from the tower. "Occupants of the Humvee identify yourselves! This is your third warning!"

Looking closer, George saw there were only four soldiers,

like at the other checkpoint. Two stayed at the tower while two were coming down the side of the embankment.

"What is it?" asked Misty.

"A checkpoint," George replied. "Just stay calm."

The two soldiers worked their way through the wrecked cars, jumped the median, and were nearing the Humvee.

"What do they want?" asked Misty.

"Probably to put us in a camp like in New Braunfels," replied George.

"Then why are you just sitting there?! Drive!" screamed Misty as she tried to force George to push the gas.

"Misty, no! They'll kill us!" he retorted.

After a moment of struggling, gunfire erupted from outside the vehicle. Misty screamed and George flinched. Both ducked down. Though they assumed it was gunfire directed at them, no bullets seemed to be hitting the vehicle. Both heard some people yelling at each other nearby. Several more shots were heard.

"Stay down," George told Misty as he looked out the window.

The advancing soldiers were no longer in sight. George looked up at the checkpoint tower. A shot rang out from the checkpoint. Someone dashed beside George's driver-side window toward a wrecked car in front of them. George flinched again, thinking it was a zombie, but watched the person with a machine gun position himself behind a car and begin firing on the checkpoint. Several others joined him, advancing on the checkpoint through the cars.

One of the soldiers tossed what seemed to be a grenade

at the people, exposing himself to gunfire. A shot ripped through his neck as he let the bomb go. Several people cleared the area as the grenade went off, budging several cars from their parked positions.

Misty yelped, then asked, "What's going on?"

"It's people shooting at the checkpoint," George whispered, shocked. "And it looks like they're *winning*."

After a brief firefight, the guard in the tower went down. Things were quiet for a moment. A voice yelled, "They're done, Abe!" George watched as four to five people stood up and started to cheer.

Misty rose from her hiding place. "Who are they?"

"I don't know yet. Could be looters. Let's just sit still for a moment."

George reached in the back for one of the weapons. An M-16. He and Misty continued to listen to the voices outside.

"Good shooting, Alex."

"Damn right."

"Dibs on that guy's gear!"

"You asshole!"

One guy ran to the bodies of the fallen near the highway. Another person ran to the tower up the hill.

"What about the Humvee?"

"I don't know. Let's go see."

George called over the Hummer loudspeaker, "Hang on, my friends. Who are ya'll?"

A voice called to them, "Don't worry. As long as you're not military or bit by deadshit, you're good."

A person stepped in front of the vehicle and stood there.

He was wearing a black flakjacket with a blue shirt on underneath and cargo pants below. He held up his hands in a peaceful gesture. Several of his buddies were getting closer, but he called to them, "Guys, get back and keep an eye out for zombies. I'll take care of this." The others walked back a little ways and started looking around.

George stepped out of the vehicle. "Stay here," he instructed Misty. "If anything happens, take off, all right?"

Misty nodded her head in agreement, but then wondered just where in the hell she would go.

George closed the door.

He walked toward the civilian, but stopped several feet short. George continued to point the machine gun at the man.

"No need for that, my friend," said the man amicably.

"Who are you people?"

"The resistance, so to speak."

"Why'd you kill those soldiers?"

"Because they've been killing *us*. Probably better than those creatures have been lately."

"Who are you?"

"My name's Abe. Listen, the commotion we started is probably going to attract some of our rotting friends. You take me and my buddies back to our base, we'll help you get wherever you need to go."

George heard a shot ring out in the distance, followed by a voice yelling, "Hey Abe, we're drawing a crowd here!" and another shot.

George thought for a quick second. Misty shouted from the Hummer, "George, they're coming!"

Knowing they were low on fuel, food, and water, George said, "All right, Abe. Let's do this."

Abe yelled to his friends, "Guys, get over here! We got a ride back!"

Things were a little cramped in the Humvee, but everybody was okay for the most part. Even though the air conditioner was on, the guys still reeked of body odor. George opened the window to let the vehicle air out.

There were four people in the back including George. One chose to man the mounted gun in back. At Abe's suggestion, George let him drive the vehicle. Misty, though still shaken in the passenger seat, warmed up to the company and became a bit more conversational. Occasionally, the man manning the gun would fire off a blast or two. Abe drove cautiously, but was doing a lot of swerving. Other than that, the ride was fairly smooth.

"So who are you guys again?" Misty asked.

"I'm Steven Gomez," one of the men answered. He wore a red bandana around his head, a gray zippered hoodie with the arms cut off, and an oversized white shirt underneath. It covered a lot of his blue jeans. He was armed with a very shiny AK-47, reminding George of the ones the A-Team used.

Steven then pointed to the other three in the vehicle. "That's Red," he said, pointing to a man with a red goatee and a head full of curls. He had on a worn-out Def Leppard shirt and carried an M-16.

"And this is Petra," he said, pointing to a woman that George and Misty originally thought was a guy.

"Nice to meet you," she said, first shaking George's hand, then Misty's. She was slender, but well built. Freckles dotted her face. She had a dirty blond mullet cut short just above the collar of her white shirt. She wore a red bandana around her neck, a buttoned blue flannel, jeans, and combat boots. She was carrying a SPAS-12.

"Mr. Hero manning the gun is Alex Rich," said Steven.

"Very cool," said George. "So what the hell's going on?"

"Well, the way we can figure it," said Steven, "It was a terrorist attack."

"Hang on guys," said Abe from the driver's seat. "Speed bump ahead."

Everyone braced themselves as the right side of the vehicle ran over something big enough to make everyone bounce in their seats. A collective "whoa" emanated from all the mouths in the back.

"Everyone all right?" asked Abe.

"Yeah, we're fine," replied Misty.

"At any rate, to what Steven was saying, *bullshit*," said Red. "It's totally obvious that it's a government plot for total control."

"Would you let me finish?" said Steven. "Then you and Alex can share your kooky theory." Red sat quiet. Steven continued, "Anyway, before the news and TV went off the air two days ago, they were reporting that terrorists had dispensed some sort of chemical and biological weapon into nursing homes across the country. Seems it sped the deaths of the old people, but brought them back. Lots of nursing home people and families, not knowing what was going on, were bit or scratched by those things, which then infected them. People were locking up their family members or strapping them down when they became crazed. But they just kept infecting people. At any rate, after it started here, it started in England, then Europe, then Asia. No word on if it got to Australia or Africa yet. Last we heard, England was quarantined, France and Germany were totally under, and Russia was holding out, but just barely."

"Probably kind of like us," said Petra.

"The president came on and said he was going to hunt down the terrorists that did this. Never mind the chaos in the streets. It was war. We don't know if he knows the group or where they're at, or even if the war started yet since the communications went down."

"Yep, FEMA has total control over the radio stations and TV now," jumped in Red. "Right now, it's mainly just a recorded message on all the channels. The movie channels are still running, though. That's cool."

"You want to tell him your theory, Red?" asked Petra.

"Oh, yeah, right," said Red.

Petra began to smile and giggle, turning to George and Misty and saying, "You're going to love this!"

"My friends, this plague is one of the final phases in the master plan of the Illuminati," Red proudly stated.

"Who are the Illuminati?" asked Misty.

"I know where he's going with this," said George. "I used to hear this kind of stuff all the time on Austin Public Access. Listen close."

"It's a secret society with ancient wisdom that goes back many centuries. Some say to the wisdom of Atlantis. Some even say to the beginning of the earth when the aliens came from Mars after a great cataclysm and created us as their slaves."

Petra started laughing. "Red, you are so full of shit! So we're all Martians now?"

Misty giggled a bit as George smiled back. "Hear him out. It's kind of interesting."

"Anyway, on May first, seventeen seventy-six, Adam Weishaupt officially created this group in Bavaria, most of its members coming from other ancient religions and secret sects."

"Did you say *sex*?" asked Petra with a laugh.

"Sex?" Abe chimed from the front seat. "Now I'm interested. Speak up, Red!"

"Not sex. *Sects*," replied Red. "Sects as in cults."

"Cult sex, Red?" Petra teased. "Boy, you are a freak!"

"Shut up. Listen, it includes the power elite of the world at that time *and* today. Some say most are even part of family bloodlines that go as far back as Ramses in ancient Egypt."

"I don't know about that," said Abe as he clipped another zombie's leg, sending it crashing into a wrecked car beside the road.

"But somebody found out about the group," Red continued. "They had to split up. They split into other groups, and disguised themselves in groups like the Freemasons, the Trilateral Commission, the Bilderbergs, and others."

"Dude, those are our world leaders. They're trying to help all the crazy shit in the world," replied Petra.

"No, they're planning our destruction and total control of the planet," Red replied. His energy became more enthusiastic. His hands were flying around as he continued to describe his theory. "See, the Illuminati ultimately see us as cattle, like slaves. They use the term 'goyen' to describe us. Their cattle."

"You haven't even told us why, though."

Abe turned a corner swiftly, rocking the passengers around for a bit.

"Hey, Speed Racer, take it easy now," said Steven.

"See, the Illuminati, they've been looking to thin the herd for years now. The U.N. even had a resolution to that effect."

"Oh yeah? Which one?" asked Petra.

"I don't know for sure, but I know they had one!"

"Right," replied Petra.

George and Misty looked at each other. George shrugged.

"So now we're in the middle of it. You want to talk about 'thinning the herd,' this is it."

"But that doesn't make sense," said Misty. "If they're using us as slaves right now . . ."

"Yeah, through the IRS system. It's a tax on the money that's lent to us through the fraudulent Federal Reserve system. The federal reserve note is issued by a private, run-for-profit corporation. It's printed for nothing and backed by nothing. It is a completely fraudulent, perpetual debt slavery instrument. It's fiat money, worth nothing. Article One, section ten, clause one of the Constitution says that . . ."

George chimed in, "The only lawful money is gold or silver. Yeah, I know exactly what you're talking about. A friend of mine used to use a competitive currency of silver and gold in Austin all the time."

"Yeah. Legal, lawful money. Not this legal tender crap!"

"Hey, as long as I get my Coke from the machine," said Petra, "those federal reserve notes are fine by me!"

"But you're only strengthening the shackles of debt slavery by using it," said Red.

"What the hell are—"

Misty interrupted, "Red, you never answered my question. Why would they want to kill us if they're using us as slaves?"

"Don't know. Maybe they underestimated the strength of this plague. I mean, the government created AIDS in the seventies and unleashed it in the eighties to try to wipe us out. And what's funny, too, is that Africa hadn't been hit by the plague, but they sure as hell are infected with AIDS."

"That's not funny, Red."

"Well, not funny, but weird in a sad way."

"Maybe less equals easier control," George volunteered.

"Conspiracies aside," Petra interjected, "I can tell you that the military was developing a kind of wound healing technology for soldiers on the battlefield."

"Sounds kooky to me," said Red.

"Shut up," said Petra. "Listen, they came up with a kind of serum that could heal the wounded. From what I heard, it was doing too good a job. It was even healing the dead to the point of reanimation."

Everyone looked at Petra.

"How do you know this?" asked George.

"When I was in the Army, they stuck me in a lab. I was a college grad in biology. After basic training, they sent me there."

"Well, those things aren't healing at all," said George. "Something is reanimating them."

"Maybe it has something to do with the oblongata, the R-Complex," said Red. "The chemical, whatever it is, reactivates that part of the brain after death. It's the part that controls motor functions. Maybe this chemical is reviving the oblongata and reanimating the dead?"

"There were some projects I caught wind of that were trying just that," said Petra. "But I never heard anymore about it after I left in '93."

"Well," said Misty, "Whoever did whatever, they really fucked the world now." She turned away in frustration and gazed out the window. Buildings were burning and there were bloody bodies everywhere.

A future in shambles.

"We should have nuked those ragheads when we had the chance," said Petra.

"You don't even know it was them. Most of the militant Arab leaders were CIA operatives. They put—"

"All right, enough of this stupid conspiracy nonsense," Petra interrupted. "Why can't we just chill for a bit and just give thanks for being alive and having a shot?"

Everyone went silent for a moment. George looked at Misty, who had begun to weep. He leaned over and held her. Steven continued to sit. Silent. Stoic. Petra munched at a chocolate bar. Red began to take notes. George couldn't figure out why.

"How much farther to the base?" asked George.

"About another ten minutes," replied Abe, skillfully

maneuvering through the streets of San Antonio, around wrecked cars, and over dead bodies.

"Where's the base?" asked George.

"Downtown. The Mercado."

The vehicle entered the base in a garage at the Mercado built in a similar fashion to the security gates of the FEMA camps.

"We stole their idea," Abe explained when George mentioned the similarity. "The real bitch was *building* it."

The walls were made of large pallets, hastily constructed, yet sturdy. On the front was a chain-linked single-hinged gate. All were crudely wrapped with barbed wire. They had built the security device in the garage, then cleared the area and pushed the gate out the garage door. They secured it to the outer wall with large bolts drilled into the stone wall.

The entrance had two doors. The first one led into a containment area. Like last time, once the front gate was shut, any zombies that got in the containment area were eliminated. Once eliminated and the containment area secured, the second, garage-style door opened.

Probably the craziest part was that the front gate had to be opened and closed manually. George and Misty watched the process from the window. Four men in what seemed to be riot gear and dog training jackets went and opened the gate for them, pulling the chain linked gate inward inside the containment area, letting the vehicle in. Their gear was stained with blood. Five zombies entered with the vehicle. Three snipers positioned above the garage were picking off the zombie intruders. Two of the men were fighting off the creatures, pushing them away from them to give the snipers a clear shot. The ones shot in the head by the snipers were dragged into the containment area as the vehicle cleared the first gate. The four men quickly began to close the gate. One man was attacked by one of the creatures that had made it in. He struggled with it as the other three men pushed against the monsters on the outside, the snipers helping them by providing headshots. The creature fighting the one man was biting into his leather-clad arm. Using the creature's own body weight and the firm grip on the leather against it, the man dragged the creature to the ground as the gate was closed, locked, and secured. Four creatures were clawing at the Humvee. The man who had dragged the zombie to the ground started stomping on its head until it cracked. He continued to stomp as the other four creatures along the side of the Humvee were shot by the snipers. The head of one of the creatures blew open right in front of George and Misty. Misty screamed and put her face in George's chest.

The gate security men then went around the containment area with a pistol and shot the creatures once more in the head for good measure. After another quick check of the containment area, one of the gate security team raised his Kevlar mask and shouted to the men at the top of the fence, "All clear!"

The garage door opened. The vehicle drove in, followed by the security team, who were dragging the bodies of the dead into the facility. Once in and the gate closed, they would carry the carcasses to the roof, where they would toss them over the side and back to the outside to rot in the warm sunlight.

The Humvee parked near several other vehicles, two cars (an Eclipse and a Tempo) and three trucks (two Dodge Rams and a Chevy F-150). There was also an Austin Police paddy wagon.

Everyone exited the Humvee.

"Man, what a ride," said George. "Thank you, Abe."

"No problem," he said, tossing George the keys.

". . . So that's what's really going on at the Yale Skull and Bones society," Red concluded as he removed his gear.

"You're full of shit, Red," said Petra.

"Anyone need a hand?" asked Alex.

"Maybe a hand*shake*," replied George, showing a smile. They shook hands.

"If ya'll need anything, you come talk to me or Red, all right? We can get you what you need."

"Thanks Alex," said George.

"And if you ever want to talk about what's really going on in the world, that's us, too!"

George chuckled, "You got it, man."

George turned around and saw the Austin Police Department paddy wagon. He grimaced in confusion.

Abe walked up to George as the others made their way into the main building. "You need to come meet our leader. He's a great guy."

"Lead the way," said George. He took Misty by the hand and followed the others into the main building.

The garage itself used to have windows, but they were now secured with boards. There looked to be several sleeping spaces in the room as well. Mexican-style blankets were in several areas on the hard concrete floor.

As they entered the main area, they walked into a plaza-type area with no roof. Old style Mexican music could be heard in the background. The light of the sky warmed their bodies as they walked across this secured mini-plaza in the direction of an old restaurant. In the distance, the moans of the dead could be heard. Several people were sitting in the area, armed with guns and drinking beer. The Mexican music became a little louder as they opened the door to the restaurant.

"*Mi Destino*," said Misty, reading the name of the restaurant from a sign over the door. "What's that mean, George?"

George paused a moment, then replied, "My Destiny."

The group went their separate ways as Abe led George and Misty to the back of the restaurant, around several corners. Windows leading to the outside were boarded up. No lights were on inside the building, but just enough light penetrated the window barriers. The creatures cast slow-moving shadows on the interior.

Abe, George, and Misty then approached two men sitting at a table in front of a door. Two handguns sat on the table in front of the men as they smoked what smelled like weed.

"Do you smell that?" whispered Misty.

"I think it's *kill*," replied George. He had learned that euphemism for pot from—*of all places*—school. One day a student, who George knew was a drug dealer, came into his junior high class halfway through a semester. Moments after the student had entered the room for the first time, another student, the troublemaker of the class, jumped up and yelled, "Man, I smell 'kill'!" Many of the students started laughing. George told the student to sit down as the drug dealer hurriedly dashed to the door. George missed him. He would have stopped him, but he was behind the over-head projector and far away from the door, trying to complete a lesson. And he was trying to get the rowdy student and the class back together again. As George finally got to the door, the student had returned, claiming he had needed to go to the restroom. George knew it was bullshit. Anyway, it was still a lesson learned, and nobody tried to bring drugs to George's classroom again now that they knew the teacher was proactive.

"Wait here," Abe instructed as he walked to the two pot-smoking sentries.

"What's going on?" asked Misty.

"Don't know," George told her.

The men looked at George and Misty. One had a very strange nose that seemed to have been broken severely at one time. He was wearing a gray athletic shirt and pants. He wore worn-in black military-style ultralites. The other man also seemed to have something severely wrong with his nose. His face was peppered with scars. George thought he might have had a bad case of acne. He was wearing what seemed to be a blue New York City fire department shirt and blue jeans with worn black shoes.

Abe waved for them to come forward. They approached the table.

As the two came closer, the man with the messed-up nose stared at George and asked, "Have we met before?"

George thought for a moment, then said, "Don't think so, man."

Before George could introduce himself, Abe said, "He's over here." The man with the scar face opened the door and let them pass through.

It was a back office area, dark and smoky. An old calendar and several nude centerfolds decorated the brown wall. A clipboard with an old schedule on it was hanging on a nail. Two folding chairs were set up against the wall.

To the right of George and Abe was a desk, and the lamp sitting there was the only thing illuminating the room. A desktop calculator, the kind that printed out from a roll of paper, was on the right side of the desk. Papers littered the tabletop. Two bottles of gin stood near the papers. A trashcan was full and nearly overflowing on the floor to the right.

Behind the desk sat a man who was taking a long gulp of whiskey. Several old cigarettes sat extinguished in an ashtray to his right, beside the calculator.

"Good sir," Abe began. "We have added some new members to our little community."

"Have we?" said the man as he turned in his swivel chair. He was wearing a gray sports coat with a black shirt underneath, blue jeans, and black shoes.

He had an eye patch over his right eye.

He stood up and extended his hand to George.

"Welcome," he said. "My name is Alphonso."

# Chapter 11

"N ice to meet you, sir," said George, extending his hand. "My name's George. This is my friend Misty."

Alphonso looked at Misty. He suavely commented, "Such a charming woman in such a horrible place. You must be tired, dear."

Misty moved toward George and gripped his arm. It was obvious that the man was creeping her out. "We're *both* tired," she said. "A little thirsty, too."

Alphonso politely called to one of the men outside, "Richardson, would you bring our guests here some bottled water?"

"You got it, boss," was the reply.

"We have plenty to eat, as this place was a restaurant just over a week ago. Before everything happened."

"Yeah. It used to be a great place," replied George. "I ate here all the time on the way to and from San Uvalde. How appropriate, huh?"

"You must be on your way there, correct?" guessed Alphonso. "Where did you drive in from? Dallas?"

"Austin, actually," said George.

Alphonso raised an eyebrow. "Ah, yes, the music capital of the world. I've spent some time in Austin. Owned a few clubs up there."

"That's cool," said George. "I always wanted to have my own place."

Richardson walked in the door. He was the one with the horrendous scars and messed-up nose. He handed some water to both of them. It was blessedly cold.

"Right out of the refrigerator, my friends," said Alphonso.

"Oh, it tastes so good," said Misty, taking a large gulp from the bottle and smacking her lips.

"Where are my manners? You two must want to freshen up. Abe, show them to the showers and give them the room in the marketplace for the evening."

"Oh, the room, sir? Very cool." Abe looked at George and Misty, and said, "Didn't I tell you this guy was great?"

"Before you go, I must share some simple rules of our little community," said Alphonso, fixing a gin drink. "*One*, kill all zombies. If they penetrate the area, we must kill them and re-secure the area. *Two*, kill all law enforcement officials." Alphonso opened a small ice chest hiding in the shadows near his desk and put ice in the drink. "Our group was formed in different areas of town. Both times we were flushed out by military personnel. Though there has not been an attack in several days, we are still wary. If you see any, kill them with extreme prejudice." Alphonso took a sip from his drink, rolling his tongue to catch all the flavor, then continued, "*Third*, kill anyone who comes close to our area. You have been allowed in as you helped transport one of our scouting teams." He placed his drink on the desk, meticulously situating it in the center of a coaster. "The final rule is to kill anyone within this base who becomes infected. This is very important." He paused for a moment, then asked, "Have I made the rules clear?"

"Yes sir," said George and Misty in unison. They understood quite well the importance of the last rule.

"While you are our guests here, you are invited to shop around the old Mercado near the room you two will be staying in for the night. We serve meals in here twice a day. Once in the morning and once in the early evening. You can snack on what you like throughout the day."

Misty commented, "Must have lots of food left in this restaurant."

"A lot indeed," replied Alphonso. "After tonight, you are welcome to stay, or we can help you get wherever you need to go. Sound good?"

George said, "Thank you, Mister . . . ?"

"Please, call me Alphonso," replied the man cordially.

"Alphonso. Thanks." George shook his hand.

"Thank you," said Misty, offering her hand as well.

Alphonso pulled her a bit closer. "And if there is anything you . . . two . . . need, just ask." Alphonso looked Misty in the eyes. Though she was nervous at the pass, she smiled.

"Follow me, guys," said Abe.

The room was at the top of a set of stairs in the Mercado area. It was a simple room with a small dresser and a large bed. The sheets weren't silk, but definitely a high thread count. The pillows were stuffed with feathers.

They stored their gear in the room and went to the showers.

The shower facility was nothing more than a room near the garage and consisted of a water hose over a large bucket. The hose came in through the window from the inner plaza area of the Mercado where there was a faucet. George grabbed his bar of soap and called for Misty to turn on the water. The water was cold, but refreshing. Misty giggled as she saw George begin to shiver. She walked around and stood by the door to the makeshift washroom.

"How's the wash?" she asked.

"It's great, but damn cold!" George replied, turning toward the door. "Don't come in."

"Didn't know you were so shy, Mr. Man." Misty giggled. She peeked through the door and looked at George.

Before she could take him all in, George called out, "Okay, turn it off."

Misty ran around and turned off the hose.

"My turn," she called out.

As the traumatic day wore on, it was obvious Misty had relaxed a bit. Though the image of the massacre was not even close to being out of her mind, it was at least in the back of it. She was feeling a little better, if only for the time being.

George sat by the faucet in fresh clothes, outside the washroom, and looked around the place.

The plaza area was secured with a crude yet effective barrier of wooden pallets, pipes, table parts and chairs on all four entrances. Primitive deterrents were along the tops of the barriers, from rusty barbed wire to broken beer bottles and glass. A brief investigation revealed that all the windows leading to the exterior had been boarded up with the same materials. It seemed effective. The base, as Abe referred to it, consisted of four large buildings. One was *Mi Destino*, the restaurant where everyone ate and drank. The building immediately adjacent to the restaurant was a two story building filled with different shops. Some sold artwork. Most were clothes and souvenir shops.

This is where George had found some clothes: a tan "Remember the Alamo" shirt and a pair of jeans.

Across the plaza were the main Mercado stores, consisting of both buildings with a hallway connecting the two. Both buildings were filled with small shops with all sorts of Mexican imports and knick-knacks.

*Not a bad prize for these people*, George thought as he looked around.

Several of the Mercado folks said hello as they passed by. There had to be close to thirty people in the group, including George and Misty. Most were well armed and seemed healthy. There had to be enough food in here to last for over a month, easily.

But there was something funny about the Mercado people that George discovered during his informal investigation. In all the areas that the Mercado people were congregating in, they were smoking. It was obviously pot. Some of the groups of people George came across were also snorting cocaine. It was beginning to look like a drug camp to George.

George returned to the faucet.

"George!" called Misty. "I got my clothes, but I forgot my towel. Could you get me one? I left it by the door."

The command took George by surprise. "Why don't you get it yourself?"

"Please?" she sighed. "Come give it to me."

George knew she was asking for the towel, but the co-quettish way she said it made him think of something else. "I'll be right there."

George ran around, saw the towel on the ground, picked it up, and knocked on the washroom door.

"I got it," said George through the door. A person from the Mercado George hadn't met yet passed him. The guy smiled, so George smiled back, a bit nervous at the obvious situation.

"Well, come give it to me. I need it."

The words shook George to the bone again. His heart fluttered a bit. She knew what she was doing. "Well, cover up, girl," he said as he walked into the room, trying to be polite.

She was crouching in the tub, modestly covering her cleavage. She had moved the hose away from the tub and it was spilling onto the floor. The natural clapping of water on stone echoed around the room.

"That's a waste of water there, young lady."

"Oh, just give me my towel," she said.

George, modestly turning his face away from her washed and naked body, handed it to her.

She took the towel from his hand and told him, "Thank you."

"Don't mention it," said George as he began to walk back toward the door.

"Hold on," said Misty.

George stopped and waited a moment. He asked, "Can I turn yet?"

Briefly wiping her body down, the water still resounding around the empty room, she wrapped the towel around her. "Come here for a second," she said.

George walked toward her. Their eyes met, though it was hard for George to ignore the cleavage of her supple breasts pressed against the towel or her shapely legs below it.

She took his hand and softly told him, "George, I want to thank you for saving my life today. I think I'm going to be a mess for a while now, in my head, you know? But I want to thank you for your bravery and for helping me today."

George was surprised, but proud at the simple accolade. "I was just at the right place at the right time, I guess," he replied. "Nothin' special, really."

She pulled him closer. His breathing adjusted to the beating of his heart. "Meet me in our room," she whispered. She gracefully leaned forward and shared a slow, arousing, and meaningful kiss with George. The room was silent, apart from the splashing water of the hose beside them.

Their lips parted.

George stood stunned.

"Well, go back to the room now. I need to clean up."

"Yes, ma'am," replied George with a smile. He walked to the door, opened it, then briefly took one last look at Misty. She was looking back at him.

"Go on, now. I'll be right there. Don't forget to turn off the water!"

"Right!"

George turned off the water, then walked to the room. Feeling fresh after the shower, he walked to the bed, sat, leaned over and laid down, his face against the pillow, and waited for Misty. It wasn't long before the general peace of the room pulled his eyelids closed.

Misty was naked.

Her breasts hung perfectly on her chest, rising and falling to her breathing. George wanted to touch her pink nipples with his mouth. She was wearing a set of white heels that accentuated her nice legs.

George chased her up a set of stairs into a room. He moved through the sheets that hung over the door. After struggling with several sheets, he entered the room. Misty was leaning on one elbow on the bed and beckoning George with the other.

George was in her arms, on top of her. Her legs wrapped around his waist. He could feel the warmth of her body. His clothes were off. He was inside her and their bodies were moving together in rhythm. A flash.

They were outside. George was behind Misty, gripping her hips and sharing himself on top of the bed. It was on a stone pedestal. She was moaning and calling his name. He reached down and gripped her breasts, continuing the motion. They felt wonderful in his hands.

A dark haired woman entered the area, naked but for a pair of high-heeled black shoes. She walked toward the couple, mounted the bed, and stood on her knees beside George and began to kiss his lips as he continued to work on Misty. George kept one hand on Misty's hip while the other reached for one of the woman's breasts. He could feel her tongue. A star burst in the sky. George looked up into the blue, then back down.

She was kissing Misty on the lips. Misty was in front of the woman, kneeling, kissing her lips and her breasts. George was under the woman, who was sitting facing away from George.

"Hurry," a voice called out.

George looked around, but saw nothing but countryside and sun.

George looked up. Misty was on top of him, facing him. George reached for her breasts again. They were perfect. He began to kiss them and stroke them with his tongue.

"Please hurry," a voice called out.

George looked around.

The sun was shining over rows of tombstones.

Misty was still on top of him. The woman knelt beside Misty and was kissing her, fondling her breasts and kissing them.

"Please hurry," the voice called out.

George looked around.

Dirt began to gather around certain areas of the tombstones, right above the area where the bodies were buried.

Misty was on her back with her legs spread. The woman was standing bent over the bed, her face working eagerly in Misty's crotch. George was behind her, looking into Misty's eyes. The women were moaning.

"Please," said the voice.

George looked around.

Zombies were rising from the graves all around them. They began to advance toward them.

George began to feel sad. He felt the voice, but couldn't recognize it.

Tears were flowing down his face.

Misty's legs were on his shoulders. He was gripping her at the crook of her hips and upper thigh. She was screaming, but George couldn't figure out if it was a good or bad scream. George began to kiss her feet, ankles, and legs as he began to cry, more of a whimper. The woman was behind him, caressing his chest and kissing his neck. She was watching Misty.

"Please stop, George. You'll be too late," pleaded the voice.

George looked around.

The zombies were climbing up toward their pedestal.

George pulled out of Misty and released her breasts and stomach. He was still crying. Misty began to giggle. The dark haired woman in the black shoes took George's sensitive area into her mouth.

"Please don't be too late," said the voice. "Please don't be too late."

George looked around.

The zombies had made it to them.

The woman looked up at George, playing with his manhood, tapping it against her lips, then disappeared.

Misty was lying on the bed. Cuddled up and asleep. She was smiling and seemed at peace. The creatures overtook the bed.

George stood alone.

Naked.

The creatures surrounded him, moments away from devouring him.

He looked to the sky.

An eye was in the sky above him. It shed a tear on a cloud.

"Please don't fail . . . Please don't fail . . . Please don't . . ."

"George?" called Misty.

George shook from his sleep and gasped.

Misty jumped. "Oh, my. Are you okay?"

"Yeah, I'm fine," he replied, wiping his eyes, removing the tears.

"So, what do you think?" Misty asked, striking a model pose.

George pulled himself together and—so as not to draw any more attention to how he looked and felt—gazed upon Misty.

She had on a dark denim miniskirt with a large leather belt. She wore a long-sleeved red mock turtleneck with the shoulders cut out as well as a generous area missing around her waist, revealing her toned stomach and belly button ring. She had silver hoop earrings and white heels with short white laced socks.

"Wow," George mouthed. "You look hot!"

"Thanks," Misty replied.

"*But*," said George, plaintively, "You're going to wear that around here—with all these guys around?"

"Oh, there's some girls, too!"

"Maybe, but still. The rules of the old world don't necessarily apply here."

"Oh, but it's so *cuuuute*," she said, making pouty eyes.

"I know, but . . ."

She came forward and crawled on the bed toward George.

*Oh my God*, thought George, who was still reclining a bit on the bed.

Misty knowingly put her hand on George's upper thigh near his genitals. She came near, face to face with him. She tauntingly whispered, *"Please . . ."*

George wanted to kiss her again, but the dream was still creeping him out. He stuttered, "Maybe you should—"

Before he could finish, she began kissing him. Her hand was slowly working its way to the area of his pants above his crotch. Soon she found his hard part and began to stroke it through his clothing.

She then pulled away from George and let go entirely.

George sighed and said, "Okay, you can wear that shopping with me, but then change out at dinner tonight."

"All right!" said Misty with excitement.

"You can put it back on after dinner, if you'd like."

"Oh, you," said Misty with a smile, as they headed down the stairs into the Mercado area.

"Where'd you get those clothes anyway?" asked George.

"Alphonso," Misty replied with a groan. "He found me as I came out of the shower room. He just offered to show me some clothes. He was acting creepy, but the clothes were nice, so I let him get away with it. Still, it's weird that he went through all the trouble of picking out an entire wardrobe for me."

"You know," said George, growing even more distressed that he couldn't recall something he felt he should, "I've never met the guy, but somehow I can't shake the thought that I do know him somehow."

"Ewww," said Misty. "I hope not."

They reached the bottom of the stairs.

"All right, let's go shopping."

# Chapter 12

The old shops were something of a disappointment, but told quite a story about the time before George and Misty walked through the door.

Most of the souvenir clothing was gone. There was lots of broken glass and objects in the floors of the shops. Ivory chessboards had been smashed. Ceramic jars broken. Cash registers mauled.

"How do you think this happened?" asked Misty.

"Good question. When things got crazy, it must have been looters at first, some trying to get into the registers, some just trashing the place."

"But why?"

"Who knows? Power. Anger. Fear. Who knows."

George could recall a time when he was young and he and some friends found an old house with the door open. Like little monsters, he remembered his friend jumping through a wall, acting silly. He remembered how much he laughed and had fun as they scurried around throwing glasses, plates, and other objects to the floor. It was a wild time.

Looking back, he understood now that it was vandalism—an inconsiderate destruction of property—of *memories*. George couldn't bear to think how he would have felt if someone did that to him or his family.

Looking at this inconsiderate destruction of property, George wondered if several young boys inconsiderately destroyed some of these shops, some of these properties, some of these *memories*. They probably laughed, not even knowing they were helping to destroy what was left of the nation.

It almost seemed, outside of the base, that there was nothing left. Nothing but rubble, charred buildings, wrecked cars, death. George was losing hope that his family was still alive.

"What do you think of this?" asked Misty, holding up a frilly wrap. "I could wear it across my shoulders . . ." She demonstrated, posing. "Or around my waist . . ." She demonstrated. Yet George was distant. "George, what's wrong?"

"Nothing, just . . . I don't know," he responded, kicking a piece of broken ceramic material across the floor.

"What? Talk to me."

"It's just . . . I don't know, there's like a weird energy flowing around here, you know? Can you feel it?"

"I can. I get a lot of it from Alphonso. It's like, he wants us to feel safe, but yet we don't? You know what I mean?"

"You're right. There's just something there. Something I'm missing. And I've been having some weird dreams, too."

"Was I good?" Misty threw out, flirting.

*If only you knew*, thought George.

"Listen," she said, tugging him toward her. "Relax. We'll be all right. And, uh, after we eat I can give you something to dream about." She reached up and kissed his lips.

George embraced her. But it still didn't feel right.

Early evening came swiftly as George and Misty finished eating. They returned to their room where they had dumped some of their stuff from their earlier bout of shopping.

Misty found some jewelry, a belt, and some practical items like a backpack for her belongings.

George found some guayaberas and a large black and white heavy cloth poncho with two horses jumping at each other.

"That food was good," said George, who had brought back a water bottle.

"It really hit the spot," Misty agreed.

"You had those guys going crazy," said George, referring to the way she looked in her outfit. She didn't change for dinner.

"Yeah, maybe. They all thought you were the luckiest man in here, though," she said as she lay down on the bed.

"Yeah, maybe," George replied with a chuckle. He took off his black guayabera and sat down on the bed, his back to Misty. He sat and thought for a moment, touching the crucifix around his neck.

"Oh," said Misty, "There you go again."

"Something's wrong here," said George, "I just feel so weird. Did you feel it again?"

"Yeah. Kind of like Alphonso and his buddies were staring at you all night?"

"So I'm not the only one. Good. I don't feel so crazy now."

She sauntered across the bed on her hands and knees, approaching George. "You're not crazy. You're a nice guy. You'll figure it out."

"I guess."

"Hey," she said, gently turning his head to face her. "You will."

George turned to answer and was met by her eyes. She was hungry for him, drawing him to her. Her icy blue eyes searched for warm comfort in the windows of George's sad soul. Like George, she desperately needed it. As she reached into his soul, it was as if his eyes were turning black.

She kissed him. He kissed her back. They began to touch each other. Shortly after, they started working their clothes off. He slid her skimpy white panties down her legs, then brought his mouth to her smoothly shaven groin and pleasured her beneath her skirt. She enthusiastically and skillfully returned the favor.

She took off her top in front of him, leaving her skirt around her hips, her earrings dangling from her lobes, and shoes clinging to her dainty feet. Her body was young and slender. Though she was soft, there was subtle development in her waist and arms, the kind earned from work. And, once penetrated, she was tight yet accommodating.

She sat down on George, holding on to his knees, and

began to bounce and grind. Her every move complemented his. She should have been the perfect distraction, but George was outside of it all, his mind troubled. As much as he had been anticipating this, he somehow could not fully enjoy the moment. Once again, a spirit returned to torment him.

Those words came across his mind again. *"Please don't fail . . . Please don't fail . . ."*

She bent over in front of him, leaning on the bed. Like clockwork, he entered her from behind, feeling more mechanical than human. He was just going through the motions. Gripping hips. Touching breasts. Kissing her mouth. Pulling her hair. Being a bit rough as her dirty words commanded.

*"Please . . ."*

The words, the whispers from his mind were upsetting him. He wanted, needed this physical moment with Misty. The voice was mocking him, teasing him, filling him with guilt.

Misty's legs were on his shoulders. He was driving into her hard and fast. She moaned with pleasure. Tears formed in George's eyes. Misty's eyes were closed, enjoying the moment and savoring every thrust, missing her lover wiping the lines of guilt from his eyes.

*" . . . don't . . ."*

The guilt was turning to anger. No matter how loud he was making Misty groan in ecstasy, it could not drown out the voice in his head.

The lovers were lying sideways together, George pressed

against her back and working from behind. He gripped her breasts, he kissed the back of her neck. His tears were disguised by his sweat.

He desperately wanted the voice to stop, to leave him alone, if only for this moment. He pulled Misty to his lips by her chin, twisting her neck. He almost felt like snapping it. He kissed her mouth like a conqueror, looking for an escape from the words, the voice in his mind. There was no solace to be found in her mouth.

Rolling her over on her belly, he pounded, holding her hands by her wrists firmly on the bed. He leaned down to her neck and bit, applying just enough pressure with his teeth, dancing on the line of pleasure and pain. It was as if he was one of the ghouls outside, the soulless zombies taking over the world. They were winning.

George knew the bite hurt, but she was too in the moment to deny him. At the height of ecstasy, it was actually bringing pleasure to her scarred soul. It disgusted George.

But the voice spoke up again, finishing its sentence.

"...*fail*..."

When she sensed him tensing up she whispered, "*You don't have to pull out.*" She was determined to give him his moment—to be accommodating. And for this George immediately felt even more guilt. Misty was convenient. He was fucking her with no emotion, denying her any sensuality or comfort she may have wanted or desired and been too embarrassed to ask for.

He was merely going through the motions.

And in a moment of release, the motions ended.

"... *Please* ..."

Misty's heart was sad. She hid the tears behind her eyes, just like she had done all her life.

George sat on the side of the bed.

Misty lay alone. Her back turned to George.

George took out Esparanza's photo and gazed at it.

"... *don't fail* ..."

The new day was beautiful. The clouds were out again, taking the edge off the spring sunshine. In a plaza across the street from the Mercado, a squirrel found some food and rushed to its nest.

Creatures continued to shamble around the city, their numbers growing.

The morning was fun and educational. Alex and Red hung out with George and Misty for breakfast in *Mi Destino* and talked conspiracies over potato and egg breakfast tacos. They talked about the Kennedy assassination being a Masonic ritual sacrifice on Dealey Plaza, named after a famous Freemason, George Bannerman Dealey. They talked about the faked moon landing, Atlantis, MK Ultra, and all the other conspiracy hallmarks. It was as if they were testing George on his knowledge. He replied and shared even more information about the deceptions by the "shadow government."

Alex asked if George needed gas for the Humvee. George said yes. Alex and Red offered to make a supply run to get George fueled up, so he agreed. Steven asked if he could tag along. He needed cigarettes.

They decided to leave at eleven. They informed the members of the compound. Alphonso was fine with it.

"Be careful, George," Misty told him. She gave him a peck on the lips. George noticed that she had become strangely reserved since their encounter last night.

He told her, "I'll be fine. Relax."

They drove out of the base and went to find a gas station.

"So how often do you guys do this?"

"Not very often," said Steven. "We've only had to make gas runs before for the vehicles you saw in the garage. We need them full in case we need to run. That was two days ago. There weren't half this many creatures out then."

"We're pulling up, about a block away," said Red, who was the wheelman. "Explain to George how we do this stuff."

"All right, I gotta make this quick so listen close. It's easy. You get out and pump the gas, Red and Alex have your back. Do you have a credit card?"

"Um, no," replied George. "I got my wallet taken from me at the FEMA camp."

"Oh, that sucks," Steven said. He reached into his own wallet and pulled out a credit card, which he handed to George. "Just use this one."

George glanced down at the card. The name embedded on the plastic in no way resembled the name 'Steven,' but George resisted the urge to question him about it. After all, what did it matter now?

Steven explained, "You'll need the card to get the gas. Now, while you're gassing, I'm gonna run in the station and try to get as much stuff as I can. So don't panic or anything if you see me rushing around. Okay?"

George felt the inherent danger and a surge of adrenaline rushed through his body. After a long exhale he replied, "Yeah, I'm good."

"All right, we're here, and a crowd is gathering," said Red from the front, pulling the Humvee into the station.

The vehicle stopped and the bullets were already flying from Alex's gun. George, Steven, and Red disembarked the vehicle. George headed to the pump. Red was capping the zombies at George's sides. Steven dashed toward the store and entered through an already broken glass door.

George entered the card at the pump. It asked for credit or debit. He pushed the credit button.

In the store, Steven shot a zombie in the head and began to grab chips, canned soups, and cigarettes. He went to the coolers and took out the last remaining cases of beer.

A zombie, the store clerk, partially devoured, rose from the office area in the back of the store. Steven was totally unaware of the creature, as he had made no effort to secure each room in the store.

Alex was mowing zombies down in front of the store.

With all the bullets flying, George realized the danger was more than just the zombies, it was the guns firing near the gas pumps. *This is absolutely crazy,* he thought, becoming more anxious now as guns continued to blaze as he waited for the pump to approve the card.

Red was effectively taking down zombies on either side of the vehicle, though the ruckus was gathering even more of a crowd.

Steven put the first armful of supplies in the truck.

The computer finally allowed gas to be pumped, so George quickly began doing so.

Steven dashed back into the store and grabbed more chips and several cases of soda.

The dead store clerk opened the office door in the small hallway leading to the bathroom in the back.

Alex reloaded. Though the machine gun was effective, the ammunition was limited. He became more frugal with the next can of ammunition.

Red reloaded both his pistols.

The zombie crowd continued gathering despite all those that had already fallen. Apparently the undead would never be fazed by the destruction of their own. Tripping and stumbling over their fallen brethren, the ghouls relentlessly pursued the hot flesh of the insurgents.

George looked at the pump. Five gallons. He pulled out his pistol.

Steven made it back and dumped his goods. He ran back in.

Eight gallons.

Steven grabbed boxes of chocolate, power bars, gum, and candy. He ran back out the door, snack items falling to the ground behind him. He threw them in the back of the Hummer and ran back in the store.

"I'm low on ammo," said Alex.

"There's an AK in the back of the truck with two magazines!" yelled Red, a little nervous. "George, get it to him!"

George left the pump and got the gun from the back. He placed it near Alex, who was still firing.

Twelve gallons.

"Get me a can!" yelled Alex, blasting away. George leaned in the vehicle and placed the cans beside him.

Red continued to fire on the advancing zombies, though an even bigger mass was fast approaching from the north.

Steven grabbed several gallons of bottled water and ran back out. He put them in the vehicle.

"Steven!" yelled Red. "One more run and we have to go! Did you get that, George?!"

"Yeah!" George yelled back. Steven had entered again.

Eighteen gallons.

Steven crossed to the back near the restroom to get some bread and canned goods. He reached down to pick up several cans of chili and beans from the bottom rack. He stood up.

As he reached for the loaves of bread on the top rack, the dead store clerk grabbed his arm and took a bite out of it. It was on his forearm, just below his elbow. Blood began to flow. He screamed, but no one heard. The gunfire was far too loud.

Steven dropped the goods and pushed the creature. It fell in the hallway. As it rose, Steven pulled out his gun and delivered a bullet straight to the forehead of the creature. It fell back to the floor. Blood splattered against a yellow "Wet Floor" sign leaning against the wall by a mop and mobile bucket.

Twenty-five gallons.

*Jesus Christ,* thought George, *How much can this thing hold?*

The creatures were closing in.

"Red! Get Steven! We need to get out of here!"

George stopped pumping and put the nozzle away.

"Steven! We gotta go!" yelled Red.

No answer.

"Steven!"

No answer.

"I'll get him," said George. As he approached the door Steven appeared, arms full of canned goods and bread. He was wearing a blue windbreaker.

"Steven, let's go," said George.

"I'm moving as fast as I can," said Steven.

Everyone jumped in the Humvee and it drove off, tires slipping and squealing from the blood oozing across the pavement. The creatures tried to follow to no avail. Stacks of the dead, peppered with bullet holes, encircled the gas station.

"Woohoo!" yelled everyone in the vehicle.

"We kicked some major ass!" yelled Red from the driver seat.

"And man, did we get a lot of goods!" George exclaimed. "Gotta love it when a plan comes together! Way to go, Steven!"

"You got it, man," said Steven.

"And look at this guy and the old school eighties windbreaker," commented George. "Where'd you get that?"

Steven hesitated for a moment, but then said, "I took it from the employees' lounge in the back of the store."

He neglected to tell them about the body that had been devoured in the back and the bite it had given him. He was sweating, hiding the pain.

"We did it, guys," said George. "Thank you all. The favor is appreciated!"

"Hey, I know I'd want help getting home, my friend," said Red. "You need to talk with me about that, too." He nervously made eye contact with George through the rear-view mirror, but quickly looked away. He seemed troubled.

"All right," said George, looking at Steven. "Hey man, take off that jacket. You look like you're burning up."

"No man, I'm fine," he replied.

They arrived back at the base before noon, still in time for breakfast.

Misty approached George and gave him a big hug.

"See, I told you I'd be fine," said George.

"I prayed for you, George. I'm glad you're back!"

"Thank you," he replied.

"Hey George," said Alex as they took their meal from the buffet-style setup. "Come talk to us later."

A little curious, but sensing a need for subtlety, George responded, "Cool. Where?"

"The garage."

"Sounds good."

Steven walked in with the cases of beer. "Hey guys, anyone want some "Natty" Light?"

Several voices from the group, many of whom George hadn't even met, called out, "Right here!" or "All right!"

After passing out several beers and getting a handshake or two, Steven started to leave.

"Hey Steven, aren't you having lunch?" Red asked.

"Nah. I'm going over to my area for a bit," he said,

sweating profusely and looking pale. Knowing he was receiving some odd glances, he added, "I had some beef jerky on the ride back and it's not sitting well."

Everyone else sat down and ate.

Outside, the creatures continued to walk around. In growing numbers.

Some were beginning to scratch at the barriers.

At around three o'clock in the afternoon, George left Misty napping in their room while he made his way to the garage to meet with Alex and Red.

"Hey guys," said George as he entered, giving them a cordial wave.

Red shook his hand and closed the door behind him. "Anyone follow you?"

"No. Why?"

"Come over here," said Alex, taking George to a corner of the room.

Red followed and they all sat down on metal folding chairs. Alex handed George a bottle of water. Red, looking nervous, stood up again and kept a keen eye on the door.

Alex stated, "We want to go with you and Misty."

"Well, that's great," said George, not wanting a change of plans, "But I'm going to San Uvalde."

"That's fine," replied Alex. "We just need to get to the intersection at 410 and 90. It's on your way home."

"What's there for you?"

"My ride," Red said. He explained that there was a storage facility just off 410 where he stored his souped-up Ford truck. Big tires. Flood lights. Grill guard. A big blue machine. He added, "We want to get it and head to Poth. I hear they've settled in and secured their city."

"Made damn near a castle out of their city hall located on their plaza," said Alex. "We hear they have about eight city blocks secured in a kind of square around the city hall." Alex took a swig from the water bottle, spat, and continued, "But get this: Inside that square was a bakery, a grocery store, and a gun shop. They're *set*, at least for another few weeks. And maybe all this will blow over by then."

"It's such a small town," said Red, "that once the outbreak occurred, they decided to meet in the center and secure the area, creating their own quarantine area around City Hall."

A glimmer of hope suddenly sprang into George's heart. San Uvalde was very much like Poth; at least the San Uvalde he remembered. George thought that perhaps they'd quarantined the city on their own and were holding out against the plague on their own terms.

"It was led by the mayor," said Alex. "He's the old school country type that called all the men to arms when infections started plaguing their city. He ignored the federal calls and edicts and took care of his people his *own* way. Bottom line, though, is they're in good shape. And FEMA hasn't tried to fuck with them yet."

"If you ask me," said George, "I don't think FEMA gives a shit anymore. They're *done*."

"You're probably right," said Red.

"But here's the other thing," said Alex cryptically, looking at Red as if Red knew just what he was going to say.

"What?" asked George, a bit apprehensive at the sudden urgency.

"I wanted to tell you at breakfast, but I didn't," said Alex.

"*What?*" George asked again.

"It's Alphonso."

"What about him?"

"We heard Richardson and Frasier talking the other day. About you."

"What'd they say?" asked George, his pulse rising.

"George," said Red, keeping a soft tone, "Did you know someone named Esperanza?"

A shot of nervousness thumped George's heart. He replied, "Yes. I had a fiancée named Esperanza—Esperanza Garcia."

Red and Alex cast a glance at each other, then bowed their heads.

George felt a lump in his throat. "What did you hear, guys?"

"George," said Alex, "You'd better take a deep breath and please, *please* think before you do anything."

George took a deep breath.

Alex said, "Alphonso was a drug dealer. The two guys with him were with the Austin Police Department. Richardson and Frasier were Alphonso's men on the inside, helping him run drugs and squash the competition."

Something in George finally clicked. Missing puzzle pieces began to form a clearer picture.

*Drug deal gone bad?*

"George, my friend," said Alex, "Alphonso and those men are responsible for your fiancée's death. They killed her. They killed Esperanza Garcia."

George sat stunned for several moments, his eyes wide, staring. Red and Alex let him sit, not knowing what more to say. Besides, how else do you tell a man that you know the person responsible for his loved one's death, other than putting it bluntly?

Though things were becoming clearer for George, there were still questions that definitely needed answers. He suddenly blurted, "I'm going to find him. I'm going to find *them*. They're going to tell me what happened." His voice got louder now. Clearer. Sterner. "And I'm going to kill him. I'm going to kill them *all*."

Red and Alex looked at each other, then again turned their faces down.

Tears began to form in George's eyes, but they were not tears of sadness. They were tears of *rage*. The shreds of his sanity were falling from the bone.

"Listen to me," said Red, "It's time for us to go. Alex and me, we're decent people. We knew Alphonso was a drug dealer, but we didn't want to leave a place where we were safe. When he first came in here, he came in that APD van with the other two guys. The back was full of pot and coke." He indicated the paddy wagon in the parking lot. "He keeps most of the others happy with his supply. Good for several months. That's why most of the people never made an effort to meet you guys or come out on supply missions. They were high. They probably don't even fully comprehend that the world's going to shit."

"*I can't believe I didn't see it,*" George mouthed, trembling as he tried to contain his anger.

"What do you want us to do?" asked Alex. "We can get the door guys now and get ready to leave. We know them. They'll let us out."

"Yes," said George. "Do that."

Red added, "We'll grab our gear and anything we want to take and pack it in now. I'll fetch Misty and send her over here. After we're packed, get the door guys and wait in the vehicle. We'll talk then."

"George, don't do anything until we're packed," said Alex. "If you're really going to kill Alphonso, we all need to be able to get out of here in a hurry. So wait until we all meet back here. Okay?"

George didn't reply.

"*Okay?*" Alex repeated.

After a moment George finally nodded, gritting his teeth.

Alex and Red looked at each other.

"Pack it up," said Red.

Alex and Red proceeded to grab their gear, which was mostly in the garage, and stuffed it all in the Humvee.

George went back to his room. Misty was not there. He went to the hall and called out for her, but received no reply. He went back in the room and hurriedly grabbed their things, then went back down to the garage and packed it in the Humvee.

"Where's Misty?" asked Red, noticeably concerned.

"She wasn't around," said George.

The gate guys were putting on their gear.

"What now?" asked Alex.

"I'm going to go find Misty," George matter-of-factly replied. "And I'm going to kill those men. Be ready to leave when I get back."

Alex approached George and extended a hand. "You be careful. Be smart. Be safe."

*Safe and swift*, thought George. He replied, "Don't worry. I'll be back."

"Take this," said Alex, handing him a .45 handgun.

George loaded the weapon, switched off the safety, and walked to the door. Without turning to face them again, he said, "If I'm not back in thirty minutes, leave without me."

# Chapter 13

The afternoon sun was shining down on the inner plaza as George exited the building and entered the concourse. Several people sat in distant corners around the plaza, smoke drifting from their mouths and wafting up into the air.

From a door in the distance, near the barrier by the Mercado building, Frasier whistled at George and signaled him to approach.

George almost lifted his weapon, but didn't want to attract attention.

Frasier ducked back into the building.

George realized that they knew what was coming. He jogged to where Frasier was and cautiously entered the building. He saw a set of spiraling stairs leading to the roof. Frasier stood at the very top, but before George could get a clean shot, Frasier disappeared again.

George took the stairs two at a time.

When he exited out a hatch at the top, he saw his three targets near the edge of the building by the street at the far end.

He didn't expect to see Misty however, with her hands bound behind her back and a gag shoved in her mouth. Alphonso had a tight grip on her hair. A large bruise was swelling up below her right eye and her face was soaked with tears. The collar of her shirt was ripped all the way down to her breasts and her bare legs were showing, skirt nowhere to be seen, her skimpy underwear protecting the last of her modesty. She was trembling.

*Please don't fail.*

Birds began to chirp in the trees of the plaza near the roof.

"George Zaragosa," said Alphonso. "I had a feeling you'd figure it out."

George pulled out his gun. The two stooges pulled out theirs. Before George could get a shot off, Alphonso yelled, "Shoot us and the girl's lunch!"

George hesitated, but continued to step forward, gun pointed at Alphonso.

"Not another step, asshole," said Richardson.

George stopped.

*Please don't fail.*

"Drop your gun and let's talk," offered Alphonso.

George let out a deep breath. No sense in a shootout. He slowly lowered his gun.

"Bring him here, guys," Alphonso commanded, motioning to his two lackeys.

They holstered their guns and approached George, then secured his hands with a zip tie behind his back, and led him to Alphonso. George stood face to face with him as the lackeys breathed down his neck from behind.

"It's kind of sad," said Alphonso. "How we have to meet like this, I mean. You seem like a really nice guy who is just a victim of circumstance—of things out of your control. Like cute little Misty here." At this point he yanked on her hair a bit, causing her to whimper. "She told me she met you at the camp in New Braunfels. You were her hero, she tells me. Do you know why she liked you when she met you, George?"

"No," said George.

"She thought you were *nice*," he said. "Isn't that nice, George? You're her hero."

George looked away. Frasier and Richardson began to chuckle.

*Please . . .*

"All her life, she had been mistreated. An abusive mother. An alcoholic father. Did you know this? Did you ever take the time to talk to her? Or were you just too busy fucking her brains out?"

George rolled his eyes in disgust.

"A sweet girl. Sweet girl, George," Alphonso said. He released his grip on Misty's hair so he could retrieve a cigarette from his breast pocket. "I made sure you found out who I was. I made sure your friends heard it from my friends." He pulled out a book of matches and lit the cigarette. "I knew it would come to this." He threw the match over the side. "The nice guy . . . the nice girl."

Misty whimpered louder.

"Esparanza was nice, too," said Alphonso. "Until she hurt my friends here, that is." Both men stood tall. Shaken, but not stirred, at the memory. Alphonso took a drag off the cigarette, then put it back between his fingers. "So I had to kill her, George."

*. . . don't fail.*

"Why?" asked George. "What happened to her, really?"

"I wanted her to work for me. I wanted to give her a better opportunity, so to speak, than she had—both with her work and with *you.*"

George growled.

"She could have had it all," Alphonso went on, "More than *you* could ever give her. A lame school teacher. Who respects teachers in America anymore? You're a dying breed."

Frasier and Richardson giggled at the comment.

"So she didn't quite enjoy my colleague's company and chose to attack them. She took their faces. She took my eye."

*Please . . .*

Alphonso paused and took another drag.

"I took her life. I shot her. It was easy to cover up. These two guys were in on a drug bust gone bad. They were injured. They got medals. She had coke in her blood. We're in the clear."

*Please don't fail.*

George was sizing up the situation. His arms were tied, he knew, but he still had his legs. But just what could he do with them?

"I had to kill her, George. She was like Misty here. *She* hurt my friends too—hurt their feelings. They asked nicely for their blowjobs, the kind they watched her give you last night. And it's only fair. After all, this is my kingdom. This is *my* castle. It's only fair that she pay restitution for being allowed to stay here." Alphonso took another drag, letting the comment sink in, then continued, "They were polite. They were gentlemen. They didn't deserve to be mistreated, George. They had no choice but to threaten her. But it turns out her blowjobs suck anyway. Literally. Not in a good way. After all, nothing's good if it's *forced*."

Alphonso was laughing as Misty screamed through her gag. Her cries came through as nothing more than a muffle. Tears continued to flow from her eyes.

George was seething. Alphonso's arrogance was burning him up inside, giving him tunnel vision. He was helpless, his hands tied behind his back, leaving only a slim chance to do anything. He wasn't ready to take that chance yet, but his anger was pushing him to do something stupid.

Alphonso looked away from Misty and focused his eyes on George again. He said, "How ironic is it that you should stumble into this place and your woman should hurt my men again?" He took a drag off the cigarette and pulled it from his mouth. He breathed out the smoke and sucked it back up again through his nostrils. "Anyway, that's how we ended up in this predicament. Some things change, but I don't. I'm the same old me."

George was sick of it. He shouted, "Enough of this shit! Fuck you and your speech! You think you're such a badass for shooting a woman?! Why don't you fucking shoot *me*!"

Alphonso burst into laughter. "You foolish dolt! I need you alive!"

George looked into Misty's eyes. Misty, teary-eyed and horrified, looked back.

"I need you alive, dear George. I need you alive to see *this!*"

With a simple shove, Alphonso sent Misty over the edge of the building, her legs flailing and her scream muted by the gag. She came down hard against the pavement ten feet below with an audible *thud*, shattering an elbow and twisting an ankle. Blood flowed like a running faucet from a large gash on her forehead, little chunks of gravel pockmarking the wound.

Zombies began to swarm around her.

George screamed, "NO!" as he lunged forward out of the grasp of the two former policemen.

Alphonso was still laughing.

People in the plaza—sitting in corners in psychedelic mindsets—all looked up when they heard the yells over the Mexican music coming from *Mi Destino*. They heard several more screams then, emanating from outside the building.

Misty tried crawling away at first, pushing herself along the ground with her good leg, but soon collapsed onto her back from the dizziness of blood loss. Her eyes fluttered, yet she remained conscious. She struggled to yank her hands free from her restraints so she could bring them out from behind her back and at least *attempt* to defend herself, but the restraints wouldn't budge. She was helpless.

The first zombie fell on top of her and bit into her cheek, then pulled away with a large chunk of stringy flesh between its teeth.

Two shots rang out.

Heads in the plaza turned.

A creature bit into Misty's leg.

A bullet penetrated Richardson's neck.

A bullet penetrated Frasier's head.

George's face was suddenly peppered with blood. A splash of crimson stained Alphonso's gray sports coat.

The thugs loosened their grip on George as they fell.

George noticed. So did Alphonso.

Someone had shot Frasier and Richardson with a cruel efficiency.

George was free to move.

A creature bit into Misty's shoulder. She was screaming through the gag still in her mouth, her muffled pleas a futile cry.

Alphonso's eyes were bulging as he reached into his jacket pocket for his gun.

George charged Alphonso, yelling nonsensical obscenities.

As Alphonso grabbed the grip of his gun, George delivered a forceful front kick to Alphonso's chest, sending the drug dealer flying over the edge of the building in one fell swoop.

George fell hard to the edge of the roof with a grunt. He looked over, his hands still tied behind his back.

Misty was being eaten alive. He could hear her softened cries. George shut his eyes and turned away.

A voice called out, "The cops, George! Get the cops!"

George looked to the roof of *Mi Destino*. Alex and Red were standing there, smoke still billowing from the barrels of their handguns.

A creature finished ripping open Misty's shirt and sunk its teeth into one of her exposed breasts. Blood pooled around its lips. She was weeping less now, her crying stifled.

Alphonso had fallen hard and awkwardly on his back, but the fall was broken by two of the zombies who were staggering toward Misty. The crowd of zombies continued to gather. Though Alphonso's back was still throbbing in pain, he tried to get to his feet.

George turned away from the sight of his friends and turned back to the cops. George picked himself up and brought his tied hands under his feet and to the front of his body. Richardson was trying to hold together what was left of his neck. Blood soaked his shirt, his hands trying to keep his head on his shoulders. His spine was the only support.

Frasier was convulsing, the headshot sparking nerves and synapses to try and find a desperate way to reconnect.

George methodically kicked Richardson in the groin, spit on his face, then soccer-kicked him in the head, snapping his neck.

He then approached Frasier. He dragged the convulsing body to the edge and pushed it over. It swirled and twirled and came down on Alphonso, who was just now up on his feet. He fell under the weight of his dead colleague.

"Take his legs out!" yelled George to Red and Alex.

As Alphonso rose to his feet again, he drew his weapon and fired on two zombies, trying to clear a path for himself. He made ready to sprint.

A shot rang out. It missed Alphonso as he continued to run away from the Mercado.

George looked at Richardson, who was done, then turned to look at Alphonso, who was running.

Another shot rang out, another miss.

George picked up Frasier's gun and aimed at Alphonso, who was moving farther and farther away, gun blazing.

*I love you, George.*

"I love you, Esparanza," mouthed George as he let an aimed shot go.

It caught Alphonso in the hamstring.

Alphonso screamed, grabbed the back of his right leg, and fell. He began to whimper as he lay on his back. A crowd of flesh-eaters gathered around him.

Alphonso took out one. Two. Three. He missed with one, but got the fourth. Fifth.

Desperate, he put the gun in his mouth.

A click.

No bullet.

He had lost track of how many bullets were in his weapon.

He tried to crawl away, but was surrounded. He fell to his back and began to cry hysterically.

A creature tore at his face. Another tore off his shirt, grabbed the flesh on his stomach, and bit. Another tore off a portion of his pant leg and bit into the meaty area above his knee. Another joined, biting and tearing at the thigh. Another did the same with the arm and sunk its teeth in. One bit into his neck. Yet another on the other leg, tearing the pant leg and biting. Another began to tug on his left leg. Another gouged out his good eye and pulled. Another bit into the neck, weakening the connection and allowing the head-puller to yank the head away from the spine, severing the connection to the brain, the remainder of the spine slithering along the ground like a snake.

More creatures began to yank at his limbs. An arm came off. Three zombies began to fight over the limb. The leg finally gave in after some twisting and gnawing. Another group was digging into his torso, removing innards and chewing on bloody organs.

Within minutes, Alphonso was devoured.

George continued to stare at the crowd gathered around the gore that was now Alphonso. A kind of satisfaction touched George—A sad satisfaction. Though Alphonso was dead, so still was Esparanza.

He looked down at Misty's remains. She had been yanked apart and torn to ribbons as well. Creatures were still tearing out organs and gristle from her torso as they splashed around in a dark puddle of crimson.

George looked away and began to cry. His whimpers turned to laughs, back to whimpers, to laughs, and back again. He was gone, swirling in a black hole of insanity.

He saw the body of Richardson, headless, now still and stiff. George's whimpers turned back to laughs as he stood up and started to kick away at the dead body. He kicked and kicked and kicked. He stomped. He jumped on the testicles of the corpse. Up and down he jumped. George pulled Richardson's gun from the holster. He shot him twice in the genitals, rolled him over and shot him twice in the ass. He sent three bullets through Richardson's spine and exploded his heart. He emptied what was left into the back of the dead officer's skull.

His laughter continued as he pulled the bloody carcass to the edge and tossed it over the side.

Another feast for the dead.

A crowd quickly gathered and began to tear and eat the flesh of the corrupt police officer. Several creatures stood below the roof, groaning with greed. Their hands were raised up high, expecting another tribute of flesh.

George found the head of Richardson. Grabbing the head by the hair, he spit into its face and began to smash it against the edge of the building. One swing. Two. Three. Laughter.

A dozen swings later, the face and head were turned to mush. George tossed the head into the street. A clump of zombies dashed onto the blacktop for the head, like children chasing down candy thrown from a float in a parade.

George turned around and saw Red and Alex standing at the entrance of the spiral staircase, staring dumbfounded at George. They had witnessed the whole of his bloody rampage. George stopped laughing. Looking at his hands, bound and bloody, he began to whimper.

He fell to his knees and continued crying.

# Chapter 14

Sanguine faces of the living dead wandered around what was left of Alphonso below a tree in the early evening hours.

A bird flew back to its nest and the three eager mouths that stood open, its children. It placed a wiggly creature in the mouth of one of the baby birds. The bird flew off, only to return with another maggot. It placed it in the mouth of the one that did not receive nourishment. It continued this process over the next ten minutes.

Food had been plentiful lately.

# Chapter 15

The morning was a bit dark, with signs of rain approaching. The sun was still shining, but clouds were beginning to gather around, seemingly determined to spoil the day.

George and Alex had explained to the Mercado members what had happened the night before. No one seemed to mind. It meant the drugs were now at their full disposal.

George, Red, and Alex ate some breakfast tacos and then said goodbye to those who mattered to them in the compound. George said goodbye to Abe and Petra. He thanked them for their help.

"No problem, my friend," Abe said. "Best of luck getting back."

George, Red, and Alex walked to the Humvee in the garage.

"You think this thing will end?" asked Red.

"Maybe," replied Alex, going to the driver side door.

"If we only knew what caused it," said George as he opened the passenger door, "Then maybe we'd have a chance."

George reached for the backseat to place his stuff.

A hand from within the vehicle grabbed his wrist. George flinched. It was Steven.

"Can I go with you guys?" he asked, his face white and sweaty.

George was surprised, but remained calm. He had an idea of what was wrong, as Steven looked like he was on his last leg: pale, cold, and stiff.

"Hi Steven," George calmly told him. "Why don't you let go of me and we'll talk?"

"I can't stay," said Steven as he began to cough. A thick glob of blood and mucus flew from his mouth and landed on George's hand.

George yanked his hand away.

"He's infected!" yelled Red.

"Get out of the truck, Steven," said Alex.

"No!" Steven cried.

Everyone knew what had to happen next.

"George, go wash your hand, man!"

George immediately ran to the faucet, turned on the water, and then went to the water room. He washed off the mess on his hand.

A gunshot resounded around the bathroom. George sighed in sad disbelief.

George found a towel and wiped his hand clean. He threw it in the trash.

He checked his hand.

There was a large scratch above his wrist on his arm where Steven had grabbed him.

The same spot where he had spit up on him.

. . .

Loop 410 was just like George remembered as they left the downtown area. The three took to the city streets around 410 to make their way to Highway 90. The Hummer was big enough to keep them secure even when the creatures tried to overtake the vehicle.

After an hour of negotiating the stalled traffic, they found Red's storage facility. The gate certainly was secure. There only seemed to be one or two creatures wandering around inside the facility.

Red entered his pass code. The gate opened. They drove in.

Several creatures entered before the gate closed, but they were no immediate threat.

They drove down several aisles of storage units until they got to the larger ones, where Alex stopped by number 1213.

"This is it," said Alex, turning to George. "Thanks for your help, my friend."

"No. Thank *you*," said George.

Red and Alex exited the truck. George and Alex guarded the sides of the storage aisle. No real threats. Only two zombies appeared, at a distance, on Alex's side.

Red unlocked the unit and opened the garage-style door.

The truck stood. Silent. Ready. It looked just like George imagined.

Red entered, fired it up, let it idle for a moment, then called for Alex.

Alex put down the two zombies on his side and walked to George.

"It was nice knowing you," said Alex, shaking George's hand.

"You too, Alex. Best of luck. Be safe."

Alex saw the scratch on George's hand. Alex looked at George.

"Take it easy, okay?" said Alex as he got into the big truck.

George moved to the driver's side door of the Hummer as Red pulled the truck out of the storage unit.

"You want me to lock it?" asked George.

"Don't worry about it," said Red. "If someone wants to go through all the trouble of looting my storage bin, then they can have at it."

"Drive safe. I'll follow you out," said George.

"All right. God bless you, my friend," said Red.

George sat in the driver's seat and put his hands on the wheel.

He looked at the scratch again. It was showing signs of infection.

George followed the large vehicle out the gate and onto the highway.

The two trucks separated. George waved to the other truck as he turned onto 90, which, thankfully, didn't look anywhere near as bad as the loop.

# Chapter 16

Rain began to pour gently over the land.

On the way to Castroville, George saw two FEMA checkpoints that had been abandoned. Stacks of nonfunctioning creatures lay beside it.

Castroville was a mess. Buildings burned. Wrecked cars. Dead bodies. Slowly, he worked his way through the city. Creatures emerged from cars and buildings and tried to pursue the Humvee. He continued to drive.

His scratch became very sore. George began to feel very warm. Sweat was forming across his brow.

The gentle rain continued to caress the south Texas countryside with water, renewing life for the spring flowers along the side of the road. Bluebonnets blossomed. Indian paintbrushes grew.

Hondo was secured by locals. George thought people were staring at him as he drove past. His scratch was swollen. Pus was covering the sore. He was very hot. Sweat was pouring over his body. He looked into the rearview mirror. His beautiful brown skin tone was slowly turning pale.

D'Hanis was another Castroville, with leveled buildings and bodies all around. Smoke was still floating into the sky from several fires around the small town.

George pulled over on the side of the road in the middle of town. His rational mental process was waning. He had drunk three whole bottles of water and needed to relieve himself. He was about to expose himself to danger as if he didn't know what was going on around him. He put the Humvee in park and exited the vehicle.

George began to relieve himself, even as the moans of the walking dead were signaling their approach. A stream of dark green urine pooled on the ground around his feet. George paid it no mind. Instead, a hunger grew in him.

When he finished zipping up, he turned back to the vehicle to find three creatures staggering around the side. Unfortunately for George, his gun was in the Hummer and he felt too sick to take on the zombies without it.

"Fuck," he said aloud, turning to run.

Creatures were coming out of the small stores and houses beside the highway, slowly chasing after George. He was feeling a lot slower, as if his body just wasn't responding to the urgency of his commands. His joints and muscles were aching.

George ran to a black car that sat in the middle of the road, the only one that was still on all four wheels and not totaled.

To his astonishment, it was a Cavalier.

The door was open. The seat a bloody mess.

The keys were still in the ignition. It was a standard transmission.

George turned the key in the ignition as the creatures closed in. The engine started, and George tried to shift to first. It stalled.

Creatures began to bang against the driver's side and passenger's side glass.

George turned the key and tried it again.

The engine started.

George shifted to first. The car sputtered, but caught. He was on his way again. He tried to switch to second, but it took several attempts as he ground the gears searching for it.

He realized then that he was losing his coordination.

The rain stopped, leaving the roads slick and wet.

Sabinal was secured by the locals. George was allowed in.

People were staring again.

His body was aching. His fever broke and George was beginning to feel cold.

He looked at himself in the rearview mirror. His face had begun to sink. Dark patches were forming under his eyes.

He pulled into a convenience store for more food and water.

As he walked into the store the clerk pulled out her weapon. George yelped and pleaded, "I'm just here for some water, please. I just want water." His voice was slurred. "I have money. There's money here." He reached into his pocket and pulled out several hundred dollar bills. Pus and blood dripped on the money. He placed it on the counter.

"I'm going to San Uvalde. Is San Uvalde alive?"

The clerk stared at George and responded, "If you mean secured, *yeah*, they're secured." The clerk lowered her weapon, though she didn't put it away.

Hope shimmered again in George's dying heart. "Thank you," he said, walking to the refrigerated doors.

He pulled open a door and grabbed three bottles of V-8, two sports drinks, a Coke bottle and two bottles of water. He dropped a V-8 bottle on the floor and started to walk out.

"Thank you, sirma'am. Have a happiness," he said. He grabbed some chips and Twinkies on the way out as well.

George exited the store and stumbled back to his vehicle.

Knippa was totally abandoned. Very few cars were on the highway now, wrecked or otherwise.

George looked in the mirror. His eyes were turning yellow. His face was sunken even more, his skin pale.

He coughed. Blood and goo entered his mouth. He spit the slime on the passenger side floorboard.

He exited Knippa.

He passed the San Uvalde city limit sign. Population 14,279.

George was trying to stay on the road. He tried to keep his eyes open. His body was in pain, but he had no energy to scream in agony. Turning the wheel and keeping control of the vehicle was near impossible now. He was driving in second gear, winding it out on several occasions. San Uvalde was in the distance. His home, on the outskirts of town, was just minutes away now.

But George closed his eyes.

His foot came off the gas.

The car stalled out as it veered off on the right side of the road and into a hill on the other side of a ditch. George's face smashed into the windshield; his left arm was caught in the steering wheel. It broke at the elbow.

A large sign stood in front of the hill before the wrecked vehicle, and in large green letters proudly proclaimed: *"Welcome to San Uvalde!"*

# Chapter 17

George opened his eyes. His vision was very cloudy. He wiped his blood from his face. He was in a lot of pain. He looked at his left arm, which dangled by his side, broken. He let out an audible moan, a vocal release of his pain. Blood dripped from his mouth as two teeth fell to the floorboard.

It took a moment for George to figure out how to get out of the vehicle, but he did. He fell to the ground.

Red ants from a nearby anthill began to attack his left hand. George decided to ignore their stings and the pain it was causing him and cry out again. It was another awkward vocalization.

George looked down the road and saw a city. He got up and began to shuffle in the direction of the city. There was a place he needed to be, but he couldn't remember where or why anymore.

George was off the road now and in the brush alongside. Every part of his body ached. It was an effort to move.

A small bird running across the highway into the brush attracted his attention. He pursued the bird. Tree branches and sharp bushes scraped at his face and body.

A small rabbit approached George. It sniffed at his foot as George grabbed it with his right hand with a peculiar swiftness.

George brought the rabbit to his mouth and bit into its neck. The animal's feet kicked as George swallowed and took another bite. The creature stopped moving. George devoured it. Blood caked around his mouth and covered his Alamo souvenir shirt.

The sun had gone up and down several times when George found a clearing that looked familiar. It was a neighborhood. It looked all but abandoned except for one house, which had lights on. George approached.

A feeling that George was unfamiliar with began to fill his body. It could be called happiness, but George didn't know what that was anymore. All he knew is that it made the ends of his lips stretch and turn upward. He coughed up some blood, but wiped his mouth again as he approached the yard of the strangely familiar house.

Another feeling came to his body. Something that could be called a memory, but George didn't know what that was anymore. He could almost see a small boy materialize on the lawn, playing "barbarians" in the front yard with sticks with his friends. Two more phantasms appeared. He saw a small boy standing next to a tall man. It's like they were taking something that could be called a picture, but

George didn't know what that was anymore. The man and the boy embraced each other. Both seemed to be dressed up for something. But George couldn't reach far enough into his mind anymore to know who anyone was or what it meant.

But he felt something pull him to the front door. A big red door made of strong wood.

He stepped on the concrete front porch.

A child, sporting a backpack and the same thing on his face that George had which stretched his lips upward, was standing on the porch and waiting. A woman embraced the child, the corners of her mouth turned upward as well.

George reached for them, but they weren't there. Somehow, he wanted that same embrace.

And now, the door. That was there. That was real. Right in front of him. His lips were stretching upward.

George knocked on the door, flesh from his knuckles breaking open on the hard wood. He winced.

A woman opened the door. George seemed to have a pleasant feeling about the woman, but he couldn't reach far enough into his mind anymore to know who she was.

George reached forward. He tried to vocalize something like, "Mom," but it came out as a guttural growl.

The woman screamed and covered her mouth.

A slender bearded man moved the woman aside and stood in front of George. He had a long, black object in his hand. Some portions of the object were brown.

"Get back everybody," the slender bearded man said.

George continued to reach forward to the man. He tried to vocalize something like, "Tio," but it came out more of a gurgling sound than anything else.

The last thing he experienced was a sudden hot blast emanating from the end of the long, black object.

His head burst into pieces.

His body fell to the porch.

*July 16th, 2004*
*Austin, in the republic of Texas*

# Director's Commentary

There was a great reality show on Comedy Central called *The Comedians of Comedy*. It was absolutely hysterical and I regret only seeing the final two episodes.

At any rate, one of the comedians, named Zach, outed a fellow comedian, named Brian, about why he was a dork. Brian was a bit surprised and upset that Zach correctly deduced that somewhere along the line a traumatic experience during their so-called "comic-book phase" trapped them in that particular phase of life, stunting their social advancement.

Granted, Brian and his comic cohort, Patton, grew up to be functioning adults, but comics are still an influence in their life.

I find myself thinking about how I got "stuck on zombies." I don't think it was anything too traumatic (or am I just lying to myself?) However, I do remember the feeling that watching the original *Night of the Living Dead* gave me, and remember the week very clearly.

It was the week of Halloween. A local television station, KABB, was going to show a week of scary movies, featuring *Halloween II*, *Prom Night*, and *Night of the Living Dead*. I must say at around this time I had a bit of a fixation on slasher movies, particularly the *Friday the 13th series.* (And yes, if I were to take a side, I'd be behind Jason all the way; Jason over Freddy every time.) Hell, there was a time when I could describe to my buddies, particularly my Boy Scout friends, most every kill from the first *Friday* up to Part 6 (which was the total at the time). I'll never forget how excited one of my friends would get when he would ask me with a smile to hear everything "right down to the blood." I didn't disappoint.

But I digress.

*Night of the Living Dead.* It couldn't be half as bad or as scary as *Halloween II* or as bloody as *Prom Night,* I thought to myself. Hell, it's in black and white. I almost didn't give it a chance, thinking it was going to be like *Creature from the Black Lagoon* or something. So I watched it and have never been the same since.

I hope if you are reading this book, you have already seen the movie. I know there's a whole new slew of fans who are appreciating the zombie genre. Brian Keene, author of *The Rising* and *City of the Dead* made a keen (no pun intended) observation to the effect of "zombies are the new vampires" in regards to popularity. I would urge any person who has not seen *Night* to find a copy of it. But there are things to watch out for:

1. Don't get the colorized one.
2. Don't get the "30th Anniversary Edition."

Most any copy that doesn't have these "additions" will give you the original black and white.

So anyway, back to the night I watched that movie. I was looking forward for some scares that week, and *Halloween II* and *Prom Night* certainly provided them to a young thirteen year old. But I didn't expect the chills, thrills, and absolute surprise when watching *Night*. What took place at the end of the movie was so stunning, so magnificent, so dumbfounding I would never look at movies the same way again. The feeling I felt during that movie is unmatched.

From that point on, George A. Romero could do no wrong.

I then found out while perusing the horror movie section of my local mom and pop video store in Uvalde that there were more Romero movies. I can't tell you which one I saw first, but I can tell you *Dawn of the Dead* made the biggest impression, story-wise. Sleepovers at my house would find us watching this one on many occasions with my friends, imagining we were the SWAT guys shooting zombies.

Yes, I was a teenager at this time. Yes, I played role playing games and made barbarians and mutant animals. Yes, I didn't have a girlfriend, either.

Yes, I'm still a dork.

(A confession. Just had to get that out of the way.)

Eventually I found on a fluke a copy of *Night*, *Dawn*, and *Day* at the local K-Mart and immediately bought them. Now, to join my copies of *Raiders of the Lost Ark* and *Temple of Doom*, were the Romero holy trilogy. *Night* still remains my favorite.

As I look back on my thirty years on this big rock, I notice that somehow I've always been writing. I was quite apt when it came to writing papers or themes in school. Even in college I loved writing papers. But it was the stories that I wrote that have always been with me. Perhaps it was the fact that my parents read to me every night, and that I became pretty proficient when it came to reading. Or perhaps it was just the active imagination of an only child. Regardless, I wrote. I wrote and drew pictures. Once I learned how to write, I began writing stories. I liked the idea of making my own stories—stories that I could be a part of. One of my earliest memories is writing one with all my friends in it. I cast them all in parts. The girls I liked got romantic roles. The boys I didn't like were the bad guys. And in the end, the boy got the girl and the bad guys were defeated. It was a very idealistic five-year-old thing to do, and I loved it.

(Man, this is becoming a bit therapeutic.)

On and off, I would write. I would always cast my friends in roles, even going so far as to put a cast of characters on the manilla page that separated subjects in the five-subject spirals. Mostly I put Indiana Jones, played by me, in typical jungle adventure roles. Later, the stories included Doctor Who and Ghostbusters.

So, on and off for close to 30 years, writing stories would be some kind of escape for me, a place where things could go as I liked—a way for me to express my inner frustrations, hopes, desires, and fears. It's art on a primitive level. More on that in a little bit.

So, *Down the Road . . .*

The story itself started around 1999. I had just got a new job as a teacher in the Hays school district. I had graduated from Southwest Texas State University (now Texas State

University) in 1998, but blew out my knee roughhousing with my buddies after a pro-wrestling pay-per-view. The ACL reconstruction sidelined me for several months and totally ruined my dream of moving to Mexico to become a luchador. I had a gimmick and everything. I was to be "El Aire: El Rey del Cielo," which basically translates to, "The Air: The King of the Skies." The reason that I was to be called El Aire is because I would be flying all over the ring with an aerial assault that would rival Jushin Liger, Kendo Ka Shin, and Rey Mysterio, Jr.

But the knee healed and I decided to make a life for myself teaching, and I got the job at Hays.

I rented a one-room apartment in Austin and lived the life of a dork bachelor, buying bootleg Japanese and Mexican pro-wrestling tapes off the internet and playing video games. When I wanted to take a girl out, I wondered why I never had any money. It all went to bootleg tapes.

So one Saturday night, I threw my K-Mart copy of *Night of the Living Dead* into the VCR and started watching it. While the movie was on, I was inspired to look for George Romero websites, as I had just got dial-up.

What I found would inspire me to write. It was a website based in England called Homepage of the Dead. It was a frickin' sweet website dedicated to the works of George A. Romero. One of the first links that caught my eye was the fiction section. I read several, with one taking place in England involving a guy who ends up running over the head of his ex-girlfriend, moving me to amazement. I thought the stories were great and should have been published.

I also thought that I should write one, with the goal of maybe, just maybe, publishing it one day. About an hour later, the first chapter was written. And for the next three years, it would languish in my computer.

A proverbial fire was lit under my proverbial ass in the form of an eccentric substitute teacher who had become a friend of mine. His name was Bruce Gilson. By some sort of fluke or divine providence, he walked up to me and in his very casual manner said words to this effect:

"You know, Bowie, a teacher at the high school just got published. She spent three months writing her book, and she got a publisher. So if you're ever writing a book, you only need to take about three months to write it."

For some reason, that statement inspired me to finish *Down the Road*. With summer quickly approaching, I knew I could finish it out before then. It ended up taking a little longer than that, but what I had hammered out was what I thought to be a very good story. Confirmation would come months later, but more on that in a while.

As I look back on the story, it was quite a vicious and lascivious tale. Once it was published, I was surprised that I even shared it with the world. I just felt it was a story that needed to be told.

I once heard advice that you should write about what you know. It was from this that I wrote a story about a teacher traveling down IH-35 to Highway 90 through the many towns I knew very well. Some parts were inspired by personal experiences, most were truly fictitious. Many of the places could be seen on a drive down IH-35. If you want to take it, you can start in Austin at 6808 S. Take IH-35 near William Cannon. Drive on IH-35 south until you hit the Kyle exit by the Burger King. Go to Koehler's Crossing to find an old middle school. Get back on 35 and take the Yarrington Road exit to get to Post Road. As you get closer to the city, you will find 1637 Post Road and the gas station just up the road from there, as well as the elementary, train tracks, and Bobcat Stadium.

Then, turn on to Aquarena Springs drive and take it to the plaza (or square, as San Marcos is not a border town like Uvalde). At the corner of Hopkins and Guadalupe is where the bat boy incident took place. Unicorn stadium in New Braunfels is not hard to find. Neither is the Mercado in downtown San Antonio. The book is like a bloody travel log for Austin to Uvalde.

And then there's good old San Uvalde. My best friend, Bo Woodman, once used the name in one of our role playing games to describe our hometown in our fantasy world. I thought it was the coolest thing, and absolutely had to use it in this story. I also plan to use the name and city as a central location for most all of my stories in the future.

Thinking about publishing, I found a group that would throw it together pretty fast. Though I knew I would be coughing up a lot of dough to get it out there, I chose to do it that way. I knew the story was very dark, very dirty, yet profound, in my opinion. I wanted to make sure it was told exactly the way I wanted it to be told, with no revisions or editors to dice it. Selfish, sure. But it was my first, and I wanted that one told my way with no concessions.

I look back and am surprised at what I wrote. Yet I'm glad that I did. Something was purged. Darkness was allowed a proper outlet for its manifestation. There's something cleansing about putting thoughts to a page, thoughts that might not be appreciated in normal conversation or social interaction. To look at it academically, that's what Art has always provided for humankind: An outlet for expression. Dennis Maganza, a theater professor at SWT that I respect very much for his knowledge of theater and life, taught me that art can be very simply defined as "any human expression." A very broad and all-encompassing definition. He also said that though it is called "art" doesn't mean you have to like it. Yet it is still an important expression to the person who created it and to anyone else who might appreciate it. If someone created it, it can be called art.

I like to think of my book as art—as my own personal expression. Many people appreciated it. Many also did not like it. I wrote it to share with all, but knew that some might not enjoy some of the more sordid and gruesome aspects.

Yet many did.

Once I put the book out to the world, it was up to me to promote it. Naturally, I went to Homepage of the Dead first. Neil Fawcett kindly offered to give one away on his site. Neil's generous offer helped me share my story with many people around the world.

It was even crazier when the first review came out of jolly old England. A member of the allthingszombie forum named Pain came out of the woodwork and was the first to review my work. I felt satisfied that his first review was very positive. It was the first of many to come. My work had been justified.

Homepage of the Dead and allthingszombie were very supportive of my works, as was Brian Keene. I am indebted to them.

On the other hand, the positive was balanced out by some negative. Some were very critical, though fair. Many offered constructive criticism. For all, I am thankful. I'm no master of writing, but I know I have many good stories to tell, and I'm glad for them to share their ideas with me to help me grow.

It took Brian Keene leaving a kind message confirming my work to know for sure that my work was legitimate. Thanks, Mr. Keene.

For all the positive I received, I began writing the sequel. As of this writing, I am currently more than halfway through. Sequel, you ask? But wasn't the end pretty final for the protagonist? Sure. But there are many people George met along the way, right?

At any rate, I hope you enjoyed this fantastic redex of my story. Special thanks to Travis Adkins, author of *Twilight of the Dead*, for taking the time to revise and polish my original story as well as open a door to a new opportunity for *Down the Road*. And thanks to Jacob Kier for giving my book the new opportunity.

To those I might have missed, believe me, you are not forgotten. Your words of encouragement, constructive criticism, and love for the zombie genre have kept me moving. Thank you so much.

And, naturally, thanks to my family for supporting my "violent, sordid tale." I'm so very lucky to have ya'll as family. I love you all. And to everyone else, Live, Love, and Be Happy.

Sincerely,

Bowie V. Ibarra